*W*hat the Critics Are Saying...

"...a heart-pounding book! I have in my hands one pulse-racing story!" ~ *Joyfully Reviewed*

"...the sexual encounters between the hero and heroine enhances the desperate mood of imminent danger which in itself is an aphrodisiac." ~ *Coffee Time Romance*

"...the author has an excellent imagination" ~ *The Eternal Night*

"The Drigon's Fall is an excellent read." ~ *Ecataromance*

Heather Holland

The Drigon's FALL

ELLORA'S CAVE
ROMANTICA PUBLISHING

An Ellora's Cave Romantica Publication

www.ellorascave.com

The Drigon's Fall

ISBN # 141995394X
ALL RIGHTS RESERVED.
The Drigon's Fall Copyright© 2005 Heather Holland
Edited by Mary Moran.
Cover art by Willo.

Electronic book Publication October 2005
Trade Paperback Publication January 2006

Warning:

The following material contains graphic sexual content meant for mature readers. *The Drigon's Fall* has been rated E–rotic by a minimum of three independent reviewers.

Ellora's Cave Publishing offers three levels of Romantica™ reading entertainment: S (S-ensuous), E (E-rotic), and X (X-treme).

S-ensuous love scenes are explicit and leave nothing to the imagination.

E-rotic love scenes are explicit, leave nothing to the imagination, and are high in volume per the overall word count. In addition, some E-rated titles might contain fantasy material that some readers find objectionable, such as bondage, submission, same sex encounters, forced seductions, and so forth. E-rated titles are the most graphic titles we carry; it is common, for instance, for an author to use words such as "fucking", "cock", "pussy", and such within their work of literature.

X-treme titles differ from E-rated titles only in plot premise and storyline execution. Unlike E-rated titles, stories designated with the letter X tend to contain controversial subject matter not for the faint of heart.

Dedication

~

To John, the man of my dreams, my source of inspiration. You've proven to me dreams really can come true, and just when you least expect them to. Thank you for helping me with my writing and understanding just how important it is to me. Love you, baby.

And to Sandy, thanks for all your help in shaping this thing up and for the *Genotites'* prayer.

Trademarks Acknowledgement

~

The author acknowledges the trademarked status and trademark owners of the following wordmarks mentioned in this work of fiction:

Lycra: Invista North America S.A.R.L. Corporation Luxembourg

The Drigon's Fall

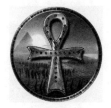

Genotites' Prayer

~

Merciful Goddess Geno, why have you forgotten your people? What have we done to incur your wrath? Since you see ill fit to gift me, your final follower, with the strength to defeat my enemy.

I shall call upon your sister the Goddess Lisk, Warrior Matron. Let my arm be strong. Help me to show this vile creature the extent of your wrath and the strength of your fury.

Help me avenge my people and with my dying breath, I give to you my soul.

Prologue

ℬ

"Computer, record," Dawson Lang ordered as he laid back on the cot in his quarters and tucked his hands behind his head as he crossed his legs at the ankles. "This is personal log number three, three, nine, nine, two of Captain Dawson E. Lang of the IPA *Drigon*."

He heard the computer beep in acknowledgement of his statement then he began recording his log. "I am currently six months and three days away from retirement after a four-year term of service in the Interplanetary Alliance, though military life was never something I had planned to partake in. When I hit rock bottom, I found myself faced with two choices—join the Alliance or join the space pirates." He paused and shifted his weight on the bed. "I look horrid in eye patches, so I opted for the more noble of the choices. If only I had known then what I know now, I may have chosen differently.

"Insubordinate. How many times have I heard that word associated with my name? So I prefer to wear jeans to the Lycra regulation uniforms. Not everyone likes that funky material, and it itches like the blue blazes." Dawson scratched his head and sighed. His choice in wardrobe wasn't the reason for this log.

"Today we find ourselves returning to spaceport to pick up the newest member of our crew—Dr. Meredith Carson. Damn General McAllister. He knows I didn't want any women onboard my ship, that's why he deliberately gave me this assignment then ordered me to not let anything happen to her. Like I have time to baby-sit the general's pet project. With my luck, she's fresh out of medical school and as green as the Nebula Eight moon."

He drew in a deep breath and let it out slowly as he sat up and swung his feet over the edge of the bed. "I guess it's my own fault, really. If I hadn't called him a spineless Jardalian, maybe he wouldn't be choosing this moment to exact his revenge. All I ever wanted was for him to leave me alone. The moment we first met, the man had it out for me. Though I suppose I didn't help it any by telling him that he had no business commanding a fleet when he obviously didn't know his left from his right hand. Of course, he had insinuated that I couldn't fly. I suppose it's a no-win situation where the general and I are concerned."

Dawson stood and paced the room. "What am I going to do about our new doctor? I don't want her onboard ship, and I certainly don't want to fly halfway across the galaxy this close to retirement on some bullshit assignment, but what choice do I have? If I don't go, I won't get that final commission I need to make renovations on the *Drigon* and get her ready for reentry into the shipping business. At least in that line of work, I don't have to deal with pompous windbags like the general."

He drew in a long breath and let it out slowly. It would do no good to get angry, and rant and rave about the general any more than he already had. "Maybe I'll get lucky and our Dr. Carson will be ugly as sin and stay locked in med lab the whole time she's here."

Dawson stuffed his hands into his pockets and moved to look out the window at the millions of stars passing by. "And there is no way in hell I could be that lucky." He turned away from the window and headed for the door. "Log complete," he said before stepping through the door out onto the bridge.

Chapter One

ಬಿ

Captain Dawson Lang peered out the observation window in his quarters. The *Drigon* circled the small planet of Ferraven, the Alliance's newest acquisition during their "expansion". They'd been sent to the planet to study it for possible use as a terra-forming station for agricultural purposes—studies showed it to be little more than a wasteland. The planet consisted of two major ice regions and a narrow band of desert along the planet's equator. As far as he could tell, the planet was useless.

Two landing parties had gone down to the planet's surface, and though signs of past life were evident in the "skeleton" forests—as the crew had dubbed them—that dotted the landscape, no life of any size, shape or form could be found. Caverns had been reported found in the southern hemisphere, though he'd refused a request to explore them. They weren't there to search for buried treasure. No, they were there on a babysitting mission, or so Dawson believed.

A woman had never walked the corridors of the *Drigon*, not until this assignment. In fact, he believed the whole assignment to be a farce for the sole purpose of keeping General McAllister's pet project safe. Doctor Meredith Carson was on her first trip into space and, if Dawson didn't miss his guess, he'd say she was a personal favorite of the general's. This was just another strike against the man.

Dawson had joined the Alliance's military four years ago out of sheer desperation. The Trade Wars had begun with no end in sight, and it was either starve or trade on the black market. The money for trading would have been better, but he didn't have much of a taste for illegal activities. From the moment he'd joined the military, he and McAllister had bumped heads. Now, three months from retirement, the old man was sticking it to him one last time with this poor excuse of an assignment.

The ship moved an almost indiscernible motion, but it was enough to catch his attention. Something wasn't right. He knew this ship like the back of his hand. She wasn't meant for military use, being a trading vessel, and soon he'd be back to the life he'd once known. Time to go to engineering, he supposed.

"Captain?" the engineer's voice sounded over the com link.

"What is it, DeVos?" he asked, pressing a button to close the observation window.

"I think you'd better come down here. Sensors indicate a fluctuation in the engines."

Dawson nodded to himself. "Yeah, I felt it. I'll be right there."

He buttoned up his jeans—they weren't regulation, but they were better than those scratchy uniform pants— and picked up his uniform jacket, sliding into it. Dawson grabbed his knife off the bedside table and slid it into his pocket. Only one person had been brave enough to make a comment on his use of what was deemed "archaic" tools and clothing. The man had ended up in the med lab having his jaw repaired. Dawson preferred his old-time jeans and tools to most of the modern technology, and most especially to the gaudy Alliance uniforms.

He stepped out of his cabin and waved dismissively to the crew on the bridge when they saluted him. They were good men, capable of handling the ship during his rest periods. He'd miss them once his term was up, but he longed for the lazy life of a trader that he'd had before.

Moving off the bridge and down the corridor, he passed the med lab on his way to engineering. Meredith was in there, and as much as he hated the thought of having a woman onboard, just the thought of that particular woman was enough to set him on edge. If he said he wasn't attracted to her, he'd be lying. From the moment the pretty little brunette had stepped aboard, he'd been fascinated with her, even though he'd tried his damnedest not to show it.

It didn't help him, or his peace of mind, that she was constantly running to him to report the findings of that damned BIOscan machine. He knew what the report was going to say before she ever opened that pretty little mouth of hers—the planet was dead. Why McAllister and the Alliance thought it'd make a good agri-station was beyond him. It was little more than a block of ice with a narrow strip of desert down the middle.

Damn his hormones. That's all it was. He was getting old and his hormones were going crazy.

Great, Dawson, sound like a woman why don't you? He ran a hand through his hair. *Well, women use that excuse all the time, why can't I? Men have hormones, too.*

He entered engineering and waved a hand dismissively at DeVos, the engineer, as the younger man jumped to attention and saluted him. "What's the diagnostics check come up with?" he asked, taking the small computer from the man.

DeVos shook his head. "Engine two's output readings are low. I'm thinking one of the circuits is shot again, sir."

Dawson nodded. "Sounds like it." He handed the computer back to DeVos and moved to the wall where he ran his finger over the sensor to open up the panel. "Do you have a replacement for it?"

"No, sir. That was the last. She seems to be going through more here lately than ever before."

Damn. He'd have to bypass it until they reached a base and he could restock on supplies. Digging into his pocket, Dawson pulled his knife out and sliced through the fiber-optic cables. He'd have to splice the cables together without the circuit between them in order to increase the engine's output. Once his retirement was up, he'd take the time to give the *Drigon* a complete makeover and completely update her.

His mind drifted to Meredith and the knife slipped, slicing into his hand. "Damn it all to hell," he swore, jerking back his hand. He flipped his knife closed and stuffed it in his pocket as he pulled a handkerchief from his back pocket and pressed it to his palm. "DeVos, finish splicing those cables back together. I need to go to the med lab and get this taken care of. Engine two's performance should pick back up after that. If it doesn't, give me a holler, and we'll figure out what the problem is."

"Yes, sir," DeVos said, saluting.

Dawson tugged one corner of his mouth up in a grimace at the man's salute and walked out of engineering into the corridor. Now he'd have to go see her—and he wasn't really sure he was ready for that just yet, though he had no real choice in the matter. The last thing he needed was to see the object of his obsession.

Damn it! I am not obsessed with her. I wish she wasn't even on the ship. Maybe my life would be a little less stressed if she wasn't around all the fucking time. Though he didn't want to admit it, he'd miss her once his three months were up.

He stormed into the med lab without so much as a hello to the woman working at a table along the far wall.

"Well, hello to you too, Captain," she said without looking up. "What brings you in today?"

"I had an accident." He plopped down in one of the chairs and waited for her to turn those pretty green eyes of hers on him.

"An accident," she began, turning to face him. She paused when he held up his blood-covered hand for her to see. "What in heaven's name did you do to yourself this time?" She moved across the room to stand in front of him. Lifting his hand, she inspected the small gash across his palm.

"I was working in engineering when the knife slipped." No need to tell her that his mind wasn't on his job at the time.

She lifted her gaze to his. Such pretty eyes set in an oval-shaped face with pale pink, perfect skin, framed in dark brown waves. Hell, he had to stop thinking like that.

"You really should learn to be more careful." Meredith reached behind her and picked up a long, narrow instrument off a tray. "I still don't understand why you insist on using such old-fashioned tools to work on the ship."

Dawson's gut clenched at the sparkle in her eyes, her dazzling smile. The woman could turn him inside out in no time flat. She took a firmer hold on his hand and drew him from his thoughts.

A warm, tingling sensation traveled up his arm from where her fingers touched him. It had always been this way, so why couldn't he find it within himself to say something to her? Damn it! Because he was a coward where Meredith was concerned, that's why.

A stray lock of dark hair fell onto her cheek and it took every ounce of willpower he possessed not to reach out and brush it back behind her ear. His body tensed with the effort, causing Meredith to lift her eyes and meet his. The bright blue light emanating from the RemLite she held ceased as she looked up at him.

"I didn't hurt you, did I?" she asked, sounding concerned.

Dawson shook his head. "No. No, you didn't hurt me. Almost done?"

He could easily get lost in the pale green depths of her eyes, but that way led to trouble. He couldn't afford to get tangled up with a woman, especially not now. In another three months, this mission would be over, and he wouldn't see her again. Retirement wasn't an easy thing to swallow for anyone, even when it was planned. But the politics were just getting too crazy. It was better to get back to the lazy life he'd led before the Trade Wars.

"I'm almost done." She depressed a button on the instrument, turning it back on. The blue light shined once more, the cut on his hand slowly fading as she moved it over the wound.

Her little gizmos fascinated him, but the woman operating them intrigued him even more — and if he didn't hurry and get away from this dark-haired little elf soon, she would know it too. Already his cock was painfully hard, and the only thing she'd done was repair his hand.

"There, all done." Her words jerked him from his thoughts and he lifted his gaze up to her smiling face.

Dawson made a fist and opened it several times to test her work. "Good as new," he remarked. "Mighty handy little gizmo you have there."

Meredith smiled. "It's called a RemLite."

"I know. We were without a doctor onboard for a while, Dr. Carson. I do know a thing or two, even if you think I'm a dinosaur," he chided.

She blushed. "Oh, sorry, sir. I didn't mean to imply such a thing."

He found himself smiling at her blush. She was definitely getting to him. The sooner he got back to the bridge, the better.

"No need to apologize. Normally a captain wouldn't have any medical knowledge." The steadiness of his voice amazed him. "I'd love to stay and talk some more, but I'd better get back to the bridge."

Turning, he left the room before she could reply. The last thing he wanted was to get caught up in a full-fledged conversation with her, though something made him pause just beyond the door. He turned and glanced back into the medical lab.

Dawson watched her from the shadows of the corridor. He needed to either get over this infatuation with her or get off the ship. Unfortunately, there wasn't much he could do about either of those options at the moment.

With a heavy sigh, he turned and headed back toward the bridge. After he checked the ship's status, he'd try to get some sleep, or at least some relief. He'd figure out which once he got to his cabin.

As Dawson stepped on deck, his men paused to look at him. They knew Meredith was giving him fits. He could see it in their eyes. He moved to his chair and sat down.

"Report." He took the ledger offered to him by the communications officer, signed off and handed it back.

"Everything on the monitors is clear, sir. Looks like another uneventful night," Hanson replied.

Dawson nodded his head. Good. Uneventful was a good thing. Boring as hell, yet good, considering their "precious" cargo onboard.

He slapped his hands down on the chair arms and pushed himself up. "Well, looks like you gentlemen have things under control. If you need me, I'll be in my quarters."

"Night, sir," they called out in unison.

He nodded his head in their direction, walked through a side door and entered his cabin.

"Lights." Instantly bright light flooded the room.

He looked over the small confines of his cabin. There wasn't much to it. A bed sat pushed up against one wall with a small nightstand next to it. He had a desk with his built-in computer terminal, and along the opposite wall, his storage compartments were found. Next to those, a door led into the incredibly small lavatory.

Dawson looked up at the ceiling and sighed. He could take yet another cold shower, which rarely helped, or he could play with his holo-shades. *Jack off in the shower or jack off with virtual stimulation.*

He hurried to his desk and flipped open the control panel. Imagination was one thing, but why fantasize when he could hear, see and feel a woman in his arms as if she was real? All he had to do was write the program, which wasn't hard at all. Besides, he had to do something to banish Meredith from his mind. The woman was driving him crazy.

Pressing a series of keys on the touch-screen, he opened up a new holo-file and set to work creating his virtual woman. First, he'd have to decide on a frame size. "Hmm, medium sounds good." He didn't want her too tall but, then again, he didn't want her too short, either.

Once he had the frame he wanted, he had to decide on features. "Green eyes. Shoulder-length dark brown hair." He looked over all his options. "Full, pouty lips and a pert little nose."

The image slowly took shape before his eyes. With a start, he realized she looked almost exactly like Meredith—maybe a little taller. He let out the breath he'd been holding. "Will I ever get her out of my mind?"

He ran his hands through his hair and smiled widely as another idea struck. Pressing another set of keys, he set to work on altering her appearance. Making her different. He was *not* stuck on her. The image began to change, the hips became more rounded, the breasts larger, the figure's legs longer. He considered leaving the changes, but reluctantly deleted the alterations. It wasn't what he wanted.

Pressing another key sequence, he opened a second file and transferred footage from video surveillance into the program. He'd just use a real image of her and edit the clothing out.

Dawson smiled. Now *that* was what he called a holo-program. He closed out the program and headed to his bed.

He jerked open the drawer and pulled out a pair of holo-shades, placing them atop the bedside table. Quickly he undressed and sat down on the bed before lying back.

"Lights." The room returned to total darkness.

Dawson slipped the glasses on, pressing a small button located at one side. Instantly he found himself gazing at Meredith's image. If she ever found out he'd programmed his holo-shades with her picture, he'd be a dead man.

* * * * *

Meredith cleaned the medical lab and shut off the lights. The corridor outside was empty, though that was nothing unusual. With the hour, most of the crew was either asleep or in the mess hall. The ship was one that could easily run on a skeleton crew, and the assignment they were on wasn't one that required a full crew to be at their stations at all times.

She slowly made her way down the corridor a short distance to her quarters. Her uncle K.C. "Kaz" McAllister hadn't wanted her to sign up with the Alliance, but she had insisted on it. All her life, she'd depended on him for everything. She was finally at an age where she wanted her independence, and joining the Alliance had been her way of proving to him that she could take care of herself. Medical degree in hand, she'd signed up right out of school, much to her only relation's dismay.

With a sigh, Meredith entered her cabin and commanded, "Lights." Instantly, the room was flooded with bright, inviting light. She looked around at the meager contents of her cabin. A regulation bed, bedside table, computer terminal and a small chair for lounging made up the cabin's furniture. Along one wall were her storage compartments and the door to the lavatory. It wasn't exactly what she'd hoped for in the way of a place to live, but it certainly beat depending on someone else for everything she needed. Besides, the *Drigon* was an older ship, so she may as well have known not to expect much.

Meredith moved to the compartment where her clothes were stored and stripped out of her uniform before pulling on her favorite robe. She then picked up her uniform and stuffed it into the cleaning compartment before closing the doors. Now to find something to occupy her time with.

She plopped down in her chair and carefully picked up the paperback book from the arm where it rested with its pages still open. Her place on the yellowed pages was easily found, though the storyline didn't quite hold her attention as she'd hoped.

Reaching up, Meredith rubbed the back of her neck. The muscles in her neck and shoulders were tense from cleaning up the lab—at least that's all she was willing to admit it was. She replaced the book on the chair's arm and leaned her head back as she closed her eyes. Her mind instantly went to thoughts of her hunky captain. The man was arrogant and he thought a woman had no business on a spaceship, but she still found him to be totally irresistible.

Just thinking about him made her burn with a deep need she'd never before known. Her body ached for the feel of his all the way down to her soul. For the very first time in her life she felt like a woman, and it was all thanks to one highly stubborn man.

Meredith sighed. How had the hard-nosed, arrogant captain wormed his way into her heart? Didn't she have enough problems with overbearing males in her life with Kaz?

Kaz. Her uncle would have a stroke if he knew about her thoughts toward Dawson. He'd never approve nor understand her choice in men. The animosity between the two was tangible, even without them being in the same room. If they did ever meet face-to-face—she shuddered. That incident didn't bear thinking about. Not to mention her feelings for the taciturn captain didn't mean squat. In three months he was retiring and she'd be reassigned to a new ship or a space station if Kaz had his way about it.

Things had a way of becoming complicated in her life and with great ease. Meredith's plans for the future never included a man, much less a stuffy ole captain, yet since she'd first set eyes on the man, all she did was daydream about him.

For as long as she could remember, she'd wanted nothing more than to become a doctor. But she had to admit—even if only to herself—that medicine really wasn't her cup of tea. If she ever had to see battle and the injuries incurred by it, she wasn't entirely sure she could stomach it. Lab classes had damned near killed her.

But that was neither here nor there. For now she was stuck where she was, because there was no way in hell she was going to admit defeat to anyone, especially Kaz and Dawson. It would please the captain to no end to learn she hated her job and was ready to leave the ship. And that was something she wouldn't do to save her life—give him that pleasure.

She rubbed her forehead. Something had to give. There was no way she could go on tormenting herself with these cloudy images of a future that most likely would never come to pass.

What she needed to do was find some way to get Dawson Lang off her mind. Her book wasn't doing the job. Maybe she could find something on the computer that would capture her interest.

She stood and placed her book in her bedside table for safekeeping. Before she closed the drawer, her pair of black holo-shades caught her eye. Well, if she couldn't find a successful way to banish the man from her mind, she could always fulfill her fantasies in virtual reality. Reaching into the drawer, she pulled out her shades and placed them on top of the nightstand—just in case.

Meredith ran her fingertip over the smooth surface of the glasses before sliding the drawer closed with her thigh and taking a seat at her computer terminal.

She ran her hand over the sensor that activated the computer and watched as the holo-screen lit up in front of her. Meredith cracked her knuckles and poised her fingers over the keys—what to look up? Her fingers flew over the sensors, showing her training in computer arts—which she'd taken at Kaz's insistence. File after file of BIOscan reports filled the screen, but there was no sense in looking at those since they all read the same. She looked into the ship's history, but the files were locked—not that she couldn't get to them if she really wanted to.

Before she realized what she was doing, she typed Dawson's name into the search box and hit enter. She read his medical history. It seemed that before her assignment to the *Drigon*, he'd rarely ever been hurt. She'd been on ship three months and he'd already been in numerous times—nearly daily. Hmm, interesting.

She scrolled through ship's logs, found his secret video game stash, then something even more interesting caught her eye—his holo-files. "Let's see what the big, bad captain fantasizes about," she murmured to herself, breaking through the security codes locking the files from outside view. Okay, so hacking was wrong, but her curiosity got the better of her.

The first program was fairly standard. Wide-open spaces filled with lush, green grasses and horses grazing in the pastures. Maybe he really was a cowboy after all. The next was of a bar with a band playing on the stage and people milling around talking or dancing on the wooden dance floor. But it was the third that caught her eye the most because her name was attached to it.

She clicked on the file and opened it, then gasped in surprised shock. There on the screen was her image— naked! What the hell? Oh, that man was so in for it. She started to get up and march to his cabin to confront him over it, but slowly lowered herself back down. What good would getting mad do? Plus, if she let on that she knew what he'd done, he could court-martial her for hacking into his personal files. Boy, did it ever suck to be her at that moment.

Meredith drummed her fingers on the desktop. What to do? What to do? A smile spread across her face as an idea came to mind. Apparently, he was thinking of her at least a little. She was thinking of him almost constantly. She glanced over at her shades by the bed. Two could play at this game.

Entering a series of commands, she directly linked her holo-shades to his using their personal access codes. Each pair of holo-shades handed out had its own individual ID tag, so tracking his down was a piece of proverbial cake.

According to the log files, he'd only just created the program a few minutes before she'd logged in. A faint beeping noise started and she turned her gaze toward her bedside table. Damn the man was fast. He was already using his shades. She pressed a series of commands into the computer just to be certain it was the file containing her information that he was accessing — bingo.

Meredith closed her computer terminal and slid from her chair. The man would never know what hit him. Slipping the robe from her shoulders, she stepped out of the fabric pooled around her ankles and climbed up onto the bed, then reached for her shades, placing them on the bed. Her pussy dampened in anticipation and her heart rate quickened.

Digging in the drawer next to her bed, she pulled out her vibrators and lubed them up. Her shades beeped again and she picked them up as she laid back. "Lights." The room went dark as she slipped on her shades, inserted her vibes and turned them on. She smiled, pressed the button on the shades' side and instantly found herself standing at the end of Dawson's bed.

Chapter Two

ဆာ

Her first sight was of large, well-shaped masculine feet with high arches and strong-looking ankles. She moved her gaze up his long, powerful legs to his erection. The rising shaft was quite long and thick, and she wondered how it would feel beneath her touch.

His hips were narrow, his chest broad and his arms muscular. Wide shoulders, a ruggedly handsome face and a head full of thick, blond-streaked hair finished off the picture.

"Come to me," he commanded, stretching out his arms to her.

Arrogant asshole.

She should refuse him. It'd serve him right if she reached up and turned off her shades, though the only one that would hurt was her. Dawson had written the program, therefore, it would run whether she was in it or not, so why deprive herself the pleasure? Instead, she moved toward him, despite her mind's protest. A niggling at the back of her consciousness reminded her it wasn't real, but her body didn't care. It felt real, a fantasy come true.

Meredith slid her body over the long length of his. The hair-roughened skin of his legs was both abrasive and ticklish at the same time. Her fingers skimmed along his hard shaft. She smiled when it jerked beneath her touch.

Leaning down, she licked his hard length and reveled in his response. To think she could cause him to shudder and moan was arousing.

She swirled her tongue around the head of his penis. Blowing gently, she smiled when his cock jerked and bounced against his stomach. Meredith opened her mouth, enveloping his erection with her lips. She played the hard flesh with her tongue, stroking it as she moved her mouth over him. Gently, she scraped her teeth over his taut flesh, sucking when he tensed beneath her.

Lifting her head, she smiled at him. How would the big, bad-tempered captain feel, or what would he do, once he learned the truth? A better question was, did she care? *No.*

"Ow!" She gasped when his large hand fisted in her hair. The hard pull stung. She moved closer in an attempt to lessen the pressure.

Meredith barely held back a gasp when he rolled with her, pinning her under his large frame. Muscles strained as he captured her hands and held them above her head. She tugged, trying to get away and he smirked at her futile attempts to free herself.

Her heart thundered in her chest as his warm breath feathered across her skin. She had no idea what he'd do next. This was his fantasy — his show.

Electrifying sensations feathered across her skin each time he kissed her stomach, blowing warm air across it. Her back arched, pressing her breasts upward when his tongue circled around first one nipple then the other. She shuddered when his hot breath washed over her breast just before he took the tight crown into the moist, heated confines of his mouth.

A moan escaped her lips as he released her hands and she delved them into his thick hair. She pulled him closer, shifting her hips beneath him in a silent plea for more. An aching need to be filled consumed her. She wanted nothing more than for him to bury his thick shaft deep within her welcoming body.

"I'm going to fuck you until you can't walk straight, Meredith," he said, his voice vibrating against her skin.

"Oh, yes, Dawson. Fuck me...please." She lifted her hips against his in desperate need, twisting and writhing beneath him.

He smiled at her words. From the sound of it, she was just as hot for him as he was for her. *Good*! This technology was something else. It made the encounter all the more memorable, though he couldn't remember programming it that way. He wanted—needed—to fuck her hard and fast. His cock was painfully erect and had been since the med lab.

Dawson trailed his hand down her body, dragging the backs of his fingers along her soft skin. Her body jerked and quivered beneath him when he inserted a finger into her sheath. He ached to bury himself balls-deep within her tight, wet pussy.

"I need you," he growled at her ear. "I want you. Do you want me?"

"Yes, Dawson, I want you...here, now. Please?" Her voice pleaded with him, indicating her need of his body.

He eased his finger from her channel and slid his hands up her sides. His fingertips rolled over the ridges of her rib cage, skimmed the soft edges of her breasts and trailed over her collarbone. He cupped her breasts, rolled the nipples between his forefingers and thumbs.

She arched her back, pressing the hard peaks deeper into his palms. He pulled gently on the pebbly flesh, enjoying the sounds of her soft moans. Bending his head, he moved his tongue in the hollow of her throat then trailed it down between her breasts. Dawson heard her breath suck in as he captured a pert nipple between his teeth and tugged.

He took his cock in one hand and spread the lips of her pussy wide open with the other. Positioning the tip at her opening, he pushed forward, inching into her slick channel. Her body slowly accepted him, inch by agonizing inch. He pushed slowly until he delivered his full length.

Dawson paused to bask in the silky smooth feel of her wet heat around him. *God, she feels so good.* He wanted nothing more than to end the charade, to go to her cabin and take her in the flesh. He couldn't do that. He didn't want her—though the program said otherwise. She wouldn't want him anyhow. His luck wasn't that good, but to have her in the flesh, to taste her skin for real…

Dawson pumped his hips, slowly pulling back, only to surge forward once more. He teased the soft skin of her neck with his tongue, swirling it over her throbbing pulse. He caressed her sides with his hands, massaged her breasts. A groan escaped his lips when she shifted beneath him, heightening the pleasure, increasing the pressure against his cock. Each thrust was like a lingering caress along the length of his shaft, causing him to push further, move harder, faster.

She tightened around him, spurring him on. He pumped again and again, feeling his come rising to the head of his shaft.

"Oh, baby," he groaned. "That's it, like that. Come for me, Meredith, do it!"

She contracted around him, her juices flowing over him in a gush. He moved harder and harder, stroked faster. "Oh, God, yes, baby."

As the last of her spasms died away, he exploded, spilling his milky, thick seed into her hot, tight, convulsing channel. He continued to rock over her until the last drop was drained from him. He lowered his forehead against hers, panting for breath.

He lifted his head and looked down into her sated eyes. Shifting his body, he reached into the drawer of the bedside table. How would she react to this one? He smiled. It didn't matter. He was on to her trickery—it was time to turn the tables.

Pulling her hands up over her head, he handcuffed her to the bed.

Meredith gasped, and he smiled. "Busted."

"What are you doing?" She tugged at her hands, unable to free them.

"I'm on to you, Meredith. I've used a holo program" he began, only to think twice about confessing to such a thing, "never mind. The point is, it was too good. Your reactions were too random. Plus, I didn't program you to talk, but that's okay. Thank you. This makes it more fun. The ball's in my field now."

"Let me go, Dawson," she pleaded, tugging at her hands once more.

"No, I'm afraid I can't do that. Not yet anyhow."

He reached up to touch the side of his glasses that she knew he wore, though she couldn't see them. "I'll be there soon, Meredith. This time, it'll be in the flesh."

Dawson depressed the button on his shades and her image faded. He jumped from the bed and headed for the shower to clean himself up. He took out some *real* handcuffs from his closet and quickly dressed. She thought him an idiot, but he'd just shown her that she had underestimated his abilities. So long as she was trapped in the virtual realm, she was trapped in reality. With her hands bound to the bed, she couldn't reach up to turn off her shades and exit the program. When he got to her cabin, he'd find her stretched out on her bed with her hands over her head, naked and ready for him. *Oh, yeah.*

He licked his lips at the thought. Nothing better than a late-night snack. He shook his head. No, she was no snack — she was the main course.

Tucking in his shirt, he grabbed the cuffs and holo-shades, slid them into his pocket then stepped out onto the bridge, nodded to his men and headed down the corridors to Meredith's cabin. Now this was going to be good, really good.

He tried to control the harsh clip of his steps, the speed with which he traveled. He wanted to draw out her anticipation...her fear. If he got there too soon, it would spoil the effect.

* * * * *

Meredith tugged at her hands to no avail. *Oh, God! Oh, God! Oh, God*! She was trapped, and he was coming to her quarters. He wouldn't really take her without her consent, would he?

Consent? Who was she kidding? She had practically waved a red flag at the man while saying "come on and take me", damn it! By being in VR with him, she'd as much as given him permission to fuck her. Hell... What was she going to do? How'd he know if he trapped someone in virtual, he trapped that person in reality too? He wasn't supposed to know these things. He hadn't shown her one shred of evidence that he knew anything about technology outside of flying this ship.

She pulled at her hands, twisting to her knees facing the headboard to achieve better leverage. Her holo-shades blocked out the real world and would prevent her from hearing him entering the room. What if he brought someone with him?

Panic shot through her like a knife, slicing at her heart and insides. Her body burned as if millions of tiny needles prickled her skin and fear dug its talons in deep.

This wasn't fair. This wasn't right, and this damn sure wasn't supposed to be happening this way. She hadn't meant for him to find out...not immediately anyhow. She'd wanted to play with him, have a little fun—then bring it to his attention that she knew of his games. Oh, crap, she was knee-deep in shit this time. If she'd just listened to Kaz when he asked her to stay home, she wouldn't be in this mess now. *But, no, you wanted to see space, travel, discover new planets. I'm an idiot.* She was too stubborn for her own good at times.

"Scared, Meredith?" his deep voice drawled at her ear.

He must have jumped back into VR to tease her some more before exacting his revenge on her. She jerked her head around, trying to peer over her shoulder. Where was he? And more importantly, what was he going to do?

He trailed his fingers up her spine, causing her to tremble beneath the gentle caress. Meredith yanked her hands once more and the cuffs on her wrists rattled.

"Let me go, Dawson."

His warm breath washed over her shoulders, his lips skimming over her skin. She closed her eyes and her body shuddered. What was he trying to do to her? Drive her crazy? His tongue swirled over the nape of her neck, his teeth scraping the sensitive skin. Well, it was working—she was definitely losing her mind.

"Dawson, come on. You've made your point. This isn't funny anymore."

"I never said I was trying to be funny, darlin', but if you insist."

"I do…I do insist. Let me go and turn the holo-shades off."

He threaded his fingers through her hair, she sighed in pleasure. "I can't let you go, Meredith, but I will turn off the shades. Besides, this position with you on your knees, facing the wall, has possibilities."

Dawson disappeared from her sight for no more than an instant before she was pulled from the VR program. She caught sight of Dawson and gasped. He was there in the flesh and totally nude!

Dawson bit back a laugh at the near-comical look on her face as confusion turned to shock—as she stared in fascination at his erection. "What's the matter, Meredith? Did I catch you at a bad time?" He watched her face turn a pretty shade of pink and the laugh he'd been fighting rumbled out.

Dawson leaned close to her ear. "Don't worry, baby. If you can take both those vibes, you can take me, no problem."

She dropped her gaze and pulled at her restrained hands. "Okay, Dawson, you've had your fun. Let me go. You can't do this."

"Why not? You hacked into my program and linked your shades with mine. In my opinion, that was an open invitation into your bed."

He watched her mouth fall open, but she said nothing. Sliding his hands down her back and over her ass, he notched up the vibes, causing her back to arch and a moan to escape her lips.

"Like that, do you?" She moaned when he pulled the vibrator in her pussy out and slowly pushed it back in. "Should I tell you what I plan to do to you?"

He removed first one vibe from her then the other. Turning them off, he placed them on the bedside table. "First, I'm going to get you all slick with this," he held up a bottle of lube and read the label. "Strawberry-scented lubricant, my favorite." Dawson waggled his eyebrows at her. "Then I'm going to fuck you hard and fast until you can't walk."

Her body trembled as he pressed himself to her back and smeared the cool gel over her skin. The sweet, aromatic smell of ripe strawberries teased his nostrils but did little to hide the scent of her arousal. He inhaled that special aroma of hot woman and desire, making his cock pulse with need. Taking his hard shaft firmly in hand, he teased her opening with the sensitive head.

Dawson groaned as he slipped inside her and then pulled back. He leaned forward, licking a trail up her back. "Want something, baby?"

"You, Dawson. I want you." She ground her ass against him and rocked back and forth on her knees. "Let me go, Dawson. I want to touch you, feel you. Please?"

He reached over and plucked the key to the cuffs off the bedside table, unlocking the restraints.

Meredith shoved back, throwing Dawson off-balance in the process. He toppled over backwards, his breath whooshing out. The key flew across the cabin to ping against the floor. She spun around quickly then tackled him, wrapping her body around his.

So, he wanted to tease her, did he? Well, now it was her turn to tease him.

She rubbed her breasts against the hair-roughened length of chest, caressing his skin with her lips, her tongue. The hair on his body was abrasive against her nipples, sending waves of pleasure fanning out through her.

She kissed his stomach and smiled when the muscles clenched beneath her touch. Meredith dragged her nails over his stomach and down his belly button, her lips leaving a moist trail in their wake.

"Meredith," he groaned when her mouth circled his cock.

"Hmm?" she murmured, refusing to move from where she lay over his legs. Her tongue swirled around the tip of his cock, causing him to shudder and groan in response. She sucked, hollowing her cheeks over the bulbous head then slid down his long cock once more. Meredith pulled her mouth from him and scattered small licks on his belly up to his chest before raising her head to look into his eyes.

"Now, Dawson, now," she pleaded, moving her hands over his chest and sides.

He rolled, pinning her beneath him, grabbed her ass and poised his cock at her entrance.

She lifted her hips into his, begging him to fill her, to complete her.

Meredith dug her nails into his back and bit his shoulder in reaction to the pleasure-pain when he pushed into her. Her breath became ragged with each thrust of his hips as she writhed under him, looking for that perfect position, the perfect fit.

"Dawson!" She wanted him closer, because no matter how tightly together they were pressed, it just wasn't enough.

"So tight, so hot," he rasped into her ear, continuing to thrust his body into hers. "That's it, baby. Come for me." He pushed harder, deeper, and she moaned again. "All for you, baby. This one is all for you, Meredith."

She cried out as the contractions overtook her. Her body quivered with each thrust of his hips and she gasped for breath.

The force of her orgasm left Meredith feeling weak and exhausted. The room around her slowly began to fade away into nothingness as she fell into a deep sleep.

It had been better than she could ever have imagined…so good.

* * * * *

Dawson looked down at her sleeping face. *God, she's beautiful.* He brushed her dark hair back away from her face. A smile crossed his lips. He couldn't blame her for being exhausted. The force of his own orgasm had rocked him to the very soles of his feet.

"Time," he called out.

"0300," the computer responded.

Dawson sighed as he glanced back down at Meredith. As bad as he hated to, he needed to get back to his own quarters, clean up and see to things on the bridge. He'd allowed this obsession with her to distract him entirely too much lately.

After the wild time they'd had, both in VR and in reality, he couldn't help but wonder why he'd fought his attraction to her so hard. His past had nothing to do with the present, and so what if she had been sent there by the man he considered his enemy? But how he felt about her meant little when he was due up for retirement so very soon. Their lives would go separate ways. Did he really want to risk his heart if it stood a chance to be broken?

Dawson skimmed his gaze over the length of her glorious form and grinned. He'd just have to take that chance. If he didn't at least try, he'd regret it for the rest of his life. With a sigh, he headed out the door to tend to his duties.

* * * * *

Meredith slowly opened her eyes. Images of Dawson still danced in her head. She'd just had the most gloriously sensual dream of her life about him and the last thing she wanted to do was to get up and go to work.

She stretched out on her bed raising her arms and yawned, her body aching in a "good way".

"Lights," she commanded, rolling to her side.

Her holo-shades lay on the bedside table. That wasn't right. She always kept them in the drawer out of sight. *How did they get...*

Memories suddenly flooded her mind. "Oh, my God." She pressed the back of her hand to her lips. "It wasn't a dream."

She vaulted from the bed, clasping the sheet to her breast and darted into the bathroom. First a hot shower then she'd go to work and pretend nothing had happened. She'd write it off as a bad dream — a really bad dream.

She quickly washed herself off. Once she was dry and dressed, she headed out into the dimly lit corridor. Attention focused on the handheld computer clutched in her palm, she was unaware of her surroundings. She should have sensed his nearness, his presence, but she didn't.

A solid wall of masculine heat materialized before her, seemingly out of nowhere. She fell back, and a pair of large hands grasped her arms, pulling her back to her feet. Her gaze slowly traveled up to his face, a face carved of stone for all the emotion it showed.

Meredith swallowed the lump that suddenly formed in her throat. Would he mention what had happened between them? Or would he act normal, indifferent? She hoped for the latter.

"Why so nervous, Meredith?"

Was it just her imagination or had his voice sounded husky? Seductive? "I'm not nervous."

He reached out and tucked a stray lock of her hair behind her ear. She flinched, and he chuckled. "You look nervous to me. Am I the cause of that?"

"Well, someone sure is full of himself. Whatever makes you think you would have such an effect on me?"

He shrugged his massive shoulders. "Oh, I don't know. Maybe the way you're trembling, or it could be the catch in your voice."

"I am not... There is not..." she began, then snapped her mouth closed. He'd baited her and, like a fool, she'd fallen for it. "Is there something I can help you with, Captain?"

He leaned close. "Yes, I do believe there is, Doctor. You see, I have some swelling that I need you to take a look at."

He took her hand in his and pulled it to his crotch. "Anything you can do for it?"

Meredith felt her face grow hot and jerked her hand away. A gasp escaped from her open mouth. "How dare you!"

Dawson touched a finger to her lips. "How dare I what? Ache for a repeat of earlier?" he breathed at her ear. "But I do ache, Meredith, more than you could possibly know, and only you can make that hurt go away. You're dreaming if you think I'm going to politely pretend nothing happened."

She shook her head. "I don't know what you're talking about, Captain."

"Don't you, Meredith? You begged me to fuck you all night. To take you over and over. Is what we did so easily forgotten?"

Meredith stepped back. He was scaring her. "This is not the place for this discussion, sir. Anyone could walk up on us. But…it was a mistake and I bear my share of responsibility. It was an avoidable situation that we allowed to get out of hand.

"Now, if you would please excuse me, I have work to do in the lab."

She started to brush past him when his hand shot out and captured her arm.

"It's not that easy to forget, Meredith, and it's far from over," he growled.

"Dr. Carson to the med lab, please. Dr. Carson to the med lab." The words repeated over the intercom system several times.

"I really have to go, Captain."

He released his grip, and she hurried down the hall. The more distance she put between them at the moment, the better. She was embarrassed and not supposed to be interested in him in any way other than professionally, yet his promise that it wasn't over sent a wave of heat washing over her. *Oh, hell, my pussy is dripping again.*

This was all wrong. He was retiring soon. The entire crew knew it. He'd want to settle into civilian life, with a civilian wife, and she was a medical officer. She wanted to be in space, yet her body ached and her heart threatened to break at the thought of him with another woman.

Damn Dawson and his arrogance...and his rugged masculinity. He had her doubting her whole life's plan and, oddly enough, it didn't really bother her. She had wanted to fly among the stars, exploring new worlds and now he had her thinking of being a wife and forgetting all about a career. Babies weren't an issue for the time being. She'd had inserted a long-lasting birth control implant before boarding ship, so at least they didn't have that complication to worry about. Though one day in the future, it might be nice to have his baby in her arms.

She shook her head. *Don't go spinning dreams, girl. Not after one encounter.*

Meredith stepped into the med lab, trying to forget about the nerve-racking man with little success. "What seems to be the trouble, Hanson?" she asked, stepping in front of the young officer.

He rubbed his left shoulder. "Combat practice. I think Bowman threw me too hard or something. I've got this terrible pain in my shoulder from hitting the floor."

She smiled at him. "That'll do it nearly every time. Why weren't you wearing your safety gear?"

"We thought it too bulky. So—"

"So you decided to forgo it. You know better than that, Hanson. That equipment is provided for this exact reason, to prevent you from being hurt."

"Yes, ma'am," he murmured, looking sheepish.

She picked up an injector and administered a dose of muscle relaxant-repairer to his shoulder. "There, that should fix it up in a few hours. Take it easy until it's had time to kick in, okay?"

"Will do, Doc Carson." He hopped down off the exam table and left the room.

Meredith sighed. She could clean the lab again—though it didn't need it—or check the BIOscan. Anything to get the captain off her mind, which was easier said than done.

Chapter Three

ର

The woman was insufferable. How could she go from the hot siren of last night to the cold fish of moments before? She was more confusing than a Cerulean mind game, and those were pretty damn bad.

A beeping sound captured his attention and he raised his head. He groaned. The damned BIOscan had just gone off...again. He hated that machine. If not for that device, he would have seen less of her and not be in the situation he was in now.

He shook his head. No, he'd be in this mess no matter what. There was just something about her that made his head spin and his body ache.

Meredith walked in, her movements drawing his gaze like a moth to a flame. She moved with such grace and poise he often wondered what a woman like her was doing on a ship with only a bunch of men for company. He would have known if she was sleeping with anyone onboard...well, besides himself, but other than last night, her record was squeaky clean. She was a mystery he intended to solve.

She walked toward him, readout in hand and a smile on her full, red lips. He held up a hand to stop her before she opened that pretty little mouth of hers.

"I don't care," he said without pulling his punches. "I can tell you what that report says—the same thing it has every other time the alarm has gone off. 'No known life forms found.' Am I right?"

One of her eyebrows shot up defiantly and she shifted her weight as she gazed up at him. "Very funny, Captain. It's part of my job to inform you of the results of the scan."

"Am I correct?" he repeated.

She threw her hands up in the air, rattling the paper she held, raising her voice. "Of course, you're right, but that's not the point."

It was his turn to raise an eyebrow. "My, my, Dr. Carson. That's some temper you've got there. Where've you been hiding it all this time?"

"That's none of your business. Permission to leave, sir."

He shook his head and crossed his arms over his chest. "Permission denied."

She smiled up at him. "Then I will take my leave since it pleases me."

He watched in shock as she took the readout and left the bridge, defying his direct order. "Damn woman," he muttered.

A snicker drew his attention and he glared at the four officers on deck. "Back to work before you're all in trouble."

"Yes, sir," they called out in unison.

"Timmons, the bridge is yours until I return." He stalked off on Meredith's heels. She wouldn't dismiss him so easily.

He moved quickly and quietly, following in her footsteps. A confrontation was about to take place, but this one would be done in private. He was already hard with need and once he started this argument with her, it would escalate into something physical — hopefully.

He watched her go into the med lab and he moved in behind her, coding the lock to the door. He wanted no interruptions for this.

"Running, Meredith?"

"From what? You?" she scoffed, allowing her gaze to move over him. "Hardly."

"What's wrong, Mere? Last night not enough for you? Frustrated? Want more?" he taunted.

She backed away from him, looking defiant. "Stop that. You don't know what you're talking about."

He smiled. "Oh, but I think I do. You ache just looking at me, don't you? Tell me what you want, Meredith."

He heard a moan escape her lips as she turned away from him. She wasn't quite so immune to him after all.

"I'm not going to sleep with you again, Dawson. It shouldn't have happened," she stated without looking at him.

"Who said anything about sleeping? I was talking about sex."

Meredith felt her face go hot. Of all the things she'd expected to hear him say, that was the last thing on her list. She turned to face him, trying to ignore her heated face.

"Captain, I hardly think this is an appropriate discussion to be having in the medical lab. I am trying to work here. Shouldn't you be off doing something, somewhere? You do run the ship, after all." Maybe that would make him leave.

He looked thoughtful a second then shook his head, smiling. "Nope, everything's taken care of. My only business at the moment is here."

"And what business would that be?"

"My business at this time is *you*."

Meredith threw her hands up and shook her head. She pointed to the door. "Out! Now! If you don't stop this behavior I'll be forced to—"

He stepped closer, crowding her. "Forced to do what, Meredith?"

She gazed up at him. She wouldn't back down, no matter what. "I don't know, but I'll think of something. I admit I was wrong to hack into your system. I admit that I participated fully. Now it's done—and it's over." She backed away from him. "No more games, sir. Let's just forget the whole thing. You let me be... I won't mention it, you won't mention it to anyone, and all will be fine."

"Who would you mention it to?" he asked.

"Dawson...Captain. Let's just forget it happened. The other crewmembers are bound to figure it out if we keep acting like this, besides I have to consider someone else. Kaz."

The mention of Kaz's name made him go red around the ears. *Did he even know who Kaz was?* If he figured out that Kaz was General K.C. McAllister, he'd be furious. She knew of their aversion for each other, which made her assignment onboard the *Drigon* trickier than it should have been. She still hadn't figured out why Kaz had assigned her to the ship of his sworn enemy.

"Are you all right?" she asked when he continued to stand there.

He shook his head. "I'm fine. Want to tell me who Kaz is and why it's so important he doesn't find out? Not that what we did was shameful. I found it quite pleasurable myself."

Damn if the man didn't look smug about it, either. "Kaz is…special. I just don't want to see him get hurt. Can you blame me for that?"

Dawson moved closer again. "Do you really want what we have to end, Mere? We're good together. Damn good together. It'd be a shame to see it end before it ever got a chance to begin. If you are worried about rank, then don't. I'm just a plain space cowboy, temporarily in service."

His words wrapped around her heart and squeezed tight. Was he talking about just sex? Or did he mean something more? Something that maybe he wasn't even aware of. The woman in her stirred to life at the glimmer of hope she'd heard in his voice, but the doctor in her demanded she remain reasonable.

The medical alarm went off, causing her to jump. She pushed past him to answer it. "I have to work now, Captain. Can we talk about this later, perhaps?"

He nodded. "Okay, Meredith. We'll talk about this later." He tugged at a stray lock of her hair and caressed her cheek. "But we're not finished, not by a long shot."

She watched him unlock the door and leave as Bowman walked in. "What can I help you with, Bowman?" she asked in a voice that was far more steady than she'd have thought possible.

"I'm just checking to see how Hanson's doing," he replied.

"He'll be fine and ready for another round tomorrow. Use your gear next time, okay?"

"Yes, ma'am." He nodded, leaving her alone once more.

Meredith sighed. Time to clean out the supply room, just to have something to take her mind off one sexy man who should be considered off-limits.

* * * * *

Well, that hadn't gone as he'd planned. Dawson paced his quarters trying to work off some of his pent-up energy. Damn, if he didn't still want her. After their earlier encounter, he'd have thought himself spent for the day.

How could she deny what was between them? And who the hell was Kaz? What was he to her? She'd succeeded in avoiding those questions. She was a puzzle he wanted to solve, and her attitude both excited and frustrated him at the same time. Damn woman.

Meredith Carson had a way of making his blood boil in more ways than one. She had the ability to turn him on in the blink of an eye, to make him go hard as a rock, but just as quickly set his temper off like no other woman could. The more he thought of her cool behavior in the med lab just a bit ago, the madder he got.

He vibrated with anger and desire. Images of her naked body wrapped around him were permanently etched into his mind. He dragged long, deep breaths into his lungs and let them out slowly in an attempt to cool the fires raging in his blood.

"Fuck it!" he growled.

He grabbed his shirt near the buttons and pulled with all his strength. Buttons flew from the fabric, bouncing off the walls. The shirt fell down his arms and dropped at his feet as his hands went to the snap of his jeans. *Well, shit, this is pathetic. I'm having a temper tantrum.*

Pausing long enough to remove his boots, he tossed them aside, then slid his jeans down his legs and stepped out of them. It didn't help. He was still on fire for her and, damn it, he couldn't have her. The holo-shades would only make matters worse now that he'd had her in the flesh.

"Lights," he commanded, stalking from the room. He entered the small bathroom. "Shower."

Seconds later steam filled the room and he stepped under the stinging spray of hot water. Dawson leaned his forehead against the cool wall of the shower stall and closed his eyes. His options were rapidly diminishing, and he couldn't see any new ones coming to fill the void any time soon.

Three months, just three more fucking months, and all his worries would be over. So why didn't he feel any better?

It was so easy to blame this all on McAllister. If the man hadn't insisted Meredith join the crew for this last mission, he wouldn't be here daydreaming about her...wouldn't have slept with her. Wouldn't know how soft her skin felt, how tight she was and how she gasped and clawed in passion.

He'd hated the man on their first meeting when McAllister had had the audacity to claim he didn't know how to fly a spaceship. He'd been flying since before he could walk. Fuck the general and his holier-than-thou attitude.

Meredith's image danced across the backs of his eyelids once more. A ragged sigh escaped his compressed lips as he wrapped his hand around his erection. He allowed himself to imagine the feel of her in his arms, of his cock buried deep within her pussy. With slow, deft movements, he moved his hand over his erection. His hand pumped harder and faster as he felt himself building to climax. He remembered how snug and wet she'd felt. When the breaking point finally came, he was thankful for the spray of water that quickly washed away his seed.

Dawson looked down at his cock in his hand and shook his head. "Damn it."

He quickly washed himself and climbed from the shower. Grabbing a towel off the rack, he rubbed his head dry with more force than necessary, but he was too pissed off to notice.

She might think it was over, but by the time he finished with her, she'd be damned sure of how much she wanted him.

* * * * *

Meredith stood in the supply room surveying her hard work. The shelves were in perfect order. She'd used the replicator to restock the things she was low on, and needed to find something else to occupy her mind until bedtime.

She exited the small room as the main doors to the lab opened. Dawson strode in looking as confident, sexy and strong as ever. His blond-streaked hair appeared to be slightly damp, as if he'd rushed through the dryer after a shower. He crossed his huge, muscular arms over his chest, stretching the fabric over the broad expanse of muscles she had recently caressed.

Her mouth went dry, her pussy grew wet and she ached to run her fingers over his skin. She pointed to the door behind him.

"I think maybe you should lock that," she said in a husky voice.

He raised an eyebrow. "Really? And why would I want to do that?"

She turned to enter one of the exam rooms and looked back slyly at him, shrugging one shoulder. "Oh, I don't know. Why don't you lock it and find out?"

She had decided during the long day that she wanted this…to take the risk. She'd tried all day to forget him and wasn't successful. It just wasn't fair that her body had more control over her actions than her brain did.

She moved deeper into the room and leaned back against one of the tables. Playfully, she opened the first button on her shirt while looking at him through lowered lashes.

Meredith watched Dawson move into the room, his gaze traveling over her body as he moved closer. She gasped when he touched her, drawing her from her frantic thoughts. He lightly traced his fingers over her face, causing her to shiver beneath the sensual caress. She leaned into him, aching to feel more than just his fingers on her face. The rigid contours of his body changed and grew harder as she pressed even closer.

Dawson spun them around, pinning her to the wall. He needed her desperately, his only thoughts of filling her and of relieving the pressure building in his cock.

He kissed her with a deep, gnawing hunger, devouring her with his lips. He greedily traced the edges of her breasts, the curves of her hips, enjoying the soft roundness beneath his palms. Dawson rotated his hips, rubbing his painfully hard cock against her. He groaned as she spread her legs—he deepened the kiss, sliding his tongue against hers in an erotic dance.

He unbuttoned her shirt, leaving the fabric to hang open. Then unclasped her bra to reveal the rounded mounds of her breasts.

Meredith moaned as he cupped her breast, palming the soft flesh. He twisted her nipple, teasing her until she writhed against him.

She moved her hand down, freeing his hard cock from its bindings. She caressed him, curving her hand around him, sliding over its length.

"I want you, Mere. Here. Now. There is no other, never was, and I think there'll never be again." Dawson lifted his head and gazed into her misty green eyes. "So beautiful, Mere. Will you have me?"

She nodded. "Oh, yes, I'm so ready," she whispered back. "But the door—"

"I locked the main doors when I came in," Dawson murmured. He lowered his head, touching his lips to hers as the alarms sounded. Frantic calls sounded over the com system, demanding he return to the bridge.

"Go," she said, pushing him away and redoing her buttons.

Dawson nodded and dashed back out the way he'd come, refastening his jeans as he went.

In the corridor, crewmen rushed to their stations. They yelled as they ran. Alarms sounded and lights flashed as he moved toward the bridge.

What the hell is going on? The ship shook, causing him to nearly lose his balance. He burst onto the bridge without breaking stride.

"Report!" he yelled, only stopping once he'd reached the controls.

"Sensors report a hull breech, sir. We're losing altitude. If we don't get her under control soon, the planet's gravitational pull will suck us in," Hanson replied in a hurried voice.

"Move," Dawson demanded, pushing the officer from his seat and sliding into the vacant chair.

Chapter Four

ഔ

No matter what Dawson did, the ship continued to plummet toward the planet's surface. Alarms sounded and lights flashed as he desperately worked the controls in hopes of a miracle, but he held out little optimism. Something had gone terribly wrong with the ship. The controls were as good as dead.

Dawson pressed on the touch screens with more force than necessary as he desperately tried to bring the *Drigon* under control.

"Fuck!" Dawson swore when more alarms sounded and the ship shimmied as it fell toward the planet. "I suggest everyone buckle down and hold on tight," he yelled. "Timmons, alert the rest of the ship to the situation."

He touched another part of the screen. "Hanson, send out an alert. We need help. Give them location and status, and do it fast." He returned his attention to the controls. There wasn't much power left in the old bird, but with any luck, there was enough to get them to the surface in one piece…or at least in as few pieces as possible.

Precious moments ticked by as the ship shook and strayed from its orbit. The planet's gravitational pull grasped the tiny vessel and sucked her in with little effort. White-hot flames licked at the *Drigon*'s hull in a fiery welcome to the planet below as Dawson held his breath.

Everything on the bridge vibrated and rattled as they hurtled through the atmosphere. Explosions sounded all around him but Dawson ignored them as he concentrated fully on the controls. He couldn't afford to worry about the men on the bridge or the rest of the ship until they were safely on the planet's surface. The ground loomed up before them, coming too fast for Dawson's taste, but all he could do was pray, even though he wasn't a religious man.

The sounds of creaking and metal ripping away from the hull assaulted his ears. Sweat poured down his face and chest until his eyes stung and his shirt was soaked.

This didn't look good.

"Shit," he muttered. "Hold together, baby. Hold together for daddy. Please hold together," he repeated over and over again. The *Drigon* had never listened to his commands and pleas in the past, but it didn't hurt to hope for a first time.

Minutes later the ship struck ground and slid across the icy surface. Sounds of the ship ripping apart could be heard, and Dawson's heart broke. His stomach lurched as the ship came to an abrupt stop with her nose buried deep in the ice and snow.

Slowly he lifted his head from the console and reached up to wipe the moisture from his brow. He held his hand out to examine it in the dim light. Blood!

"Damn it. Can't a guy get a break around here?" He wiped his forehead on his sleeve and winced in pain. "Fuck!" The damn thing probably needed immediate medical attention, and with his luck, Meredith had been injured in the crash.

Meredith! Oh, God, let her be okay. He couldn't lose her now. Finding her was foremost on his to-do list. He had to be certain she was alive and unhurt.

Dawson pulled himself up and checked the status of his men. Hanson was on his feet and helped him to dig the other three officers from the wreckage.

"Stay here. I'm going to look over the rest of the ship to assess the damage and check on the crew." He nodded toward the supine men. "How are they?"

"Looks like we lost Lt. Casavont and Morgan is barely hanging on. I doubt he'll make it until Dr. Carson arrives. Timmons is okay, sir. Just a few bumps and scratches like us."

Dawson nodded and headed off the bridge, making his way toward the med lab and Meredith. Wires hung down from the ceiling, and sparks popped and crackled as he carefully maneuvered through the maze.

He tripped over something, and his gaze darted down to see what it was. The flashing orange and red lights had died, but he could still see well enough to cause a stab of pain through him at the sight. A black regulation boot stuck out from beneath a pile of rubble. He squeezed his eyes shut for a sec before pulling debris from the buried man.

"Hanson, man down in the corridor!" He yelled for assistance.

The bulkhead had collapsed, scattering the cargo inside all over the corridor. Dawson tossed panels and the supply crates over his shoulders as he quickly dug out the unknown crewman, all the while hoping the man was alive.

His breath sucked in as he removed the last panel. Blood covered the man's face, obscuring his features from view. Reluctantly, he reached forward and checked for a pulse...nothing. He'd been too late.

"Damn it. Why is this happening now of all times? Three fucking months from retirement!" He turned away from the mangled body and kicked a large canister from his path. "This is all McAllister's fault. When we get back to Omega Six, I am going to kick his ass for it."

Two crewmen were dead, one as good as dead, no telling how many others, and he hated to think of injuries, especially if Meredith hadn't made it.

Meredith. Damn it. He had too many things bombarding his mind at once. Finding the dead crewman had momentarily removed her from his mind. *She'll be beautiful and unharmed when I find her.* It was an irrational thought, but it kept him moving. He continued to wade through the debris to the back compartments of the ship.

Halfway to the medical lab, he paused. Grief washed over him when he discovered a large section of the ship missing. The ripping sounds had been an entire section of the ship breaking apart.

Damn it! This was getting worse by the minute, though he could at least be thankful for the breathable air. He had to find Meredith, and he had to find her now.

He ran across the expanse of snow between the segments of the ship. Several feet separated the two sections, and various pieces of twisted metal littered the ground between them.

The med lab doors were sealed tight, and Dawson found himself breathing a sigh of relief and hope. If the doors were shut, maybe that meant whoever was inside was safe. Meredith had to be fine.

He pushed, tugged and tried to pry his fingers between the double sliding doors. The huge metal doors refused to budge at first, but then slowly parted only a bit—but it was enough. Pulling outward in both directions, he managed to widen the space.

Dawson was so caught up in his efforts that he almost missed the tingle in his hands when something warm and soft brushed against his fingers, then the door suddenly burst open.

He allowed his hands to fall and breathed a sigh of relief. Meredith stood before him—somewhat frazzled, but to his eyes, more beautiful than ever. It took every ounce of willpower he possessed not to pull her into his arms.

Blood trickled down his face, he was tired and his men needed a leader more than ever, yet he still felt himself hardening at the mere sight of her. He cursed himself under his breath for being such a besotted fool.

Shaking himself out of his moment of weakness, he looked around him for the first time. Two men, Temple and Ainsley, stood around dazed from the events that had unfolded. Already, he felt the cold seeping in from outside the doors.

He pulled his gaze from Meredith and began barking orders. "Someone close those doors until we get the supplies gathered that we'll need." He turned back to Meredith. "Is the replicator still working by any chance?" The lights were already flickering, but they'd need coats if they were to survive the harsh conditions of the planet.

She nodded. "So long as the lab's power holds up, but I'm not sure how long that'll be. I'll get right on it."

Meredith dashed over to the replicator and set to work creating the necessary supplies while she could. Pressing a series of buttons, she set it to create coats, blankets and any other snow-cold climate gear she could find in its database. She glanced over her shoulder to watch Dawson, sadness nearly choking her. He stood across the room, speaking to the men. After he finished giving orders, he sat on one of the tables. The doors to the lab slid open as Hanson and Timmons walked in carrying a downed man between them. Hanson paused to help Temple push the doors closed once more behind them. Meredith nodded at Hanson who walked over to join her.

"Hanson, I need to see to Ferreti and the captain needs medical attention as well. Could you please finish making the coats and blankets before the power gives out completely?"

"Sure thing, ma'am," he replied, stepping between her and the replicator.

Meredith gave him a weak smile. "Thanks. I'll tend your wounds and the others as soon as I can."

She moved across the cluttered floor to Dawson's side and touched his brow. He flinched at her touch, but she chalked it up to the area being tender. She gazed around the floor until she found her RemLite and picked it up then proceeded to heal his wound.

"Anyone know the status of the crew? Who's left?" he asked as she worked.

Meredith paused in running the RemLite over his wounds. "We lost at least one when the hull broke apart. I tried to pull him into the lab before the doors shut, but...but I couldn't."

"You did everything you could. That's all anyone can ask of you. It's not your fault…it's mine," he said, reaching up to brush her hair from her face.

She shook her head. "It's no more your fault than it's mine, Dawson. Any idea what went wrong?" Meredith motioned one of the walking wounded to her side and went to work repairing his wounds. She glanced over her shoulder at Dawson. "Were we attacked? Was the ship hit by enemy fire?"

Dawson shook his head. "I'm not sure what happened, but there wasn't another ship in this area. We were alone." He sighed and ran his hand through his hair.

He turned his attention to the door as two men walked in, each carrying a downed man in a fireman's lift over their shoulders. "Report," he called out. Their grim expressions said more than words could have.

"It's not good, sir."

"How many casualties, Jacobs?" Dawson asked.

"It may be easier to ask how many survivors, sir," the crewman replied. "Regan and Santos are both critically injured. I doubt Dr. Carson can do anything with most of her equipment destroyed, and we lost Lt. Morgan. We were preparing him for transport when he — passed."

Meredith glanced at the wounded men. "I'll see what I can do."

"Anyone seen DeVos?" Dawson asked, shifting his gaze from one crewmember to the next.

"No, sir. Engineering is a mess. The hull was probably damaged before we hit the atmosphere and the trip down ripped her to shreds," Hanson answered in a grim tone.

Dawson sighed. DeVos had been a good kid. He shifted his gaze and watched as Meredith set to work tending to his men, assessing their injuries, mending the ones she could. His hand moved up to absently rub the spot she had just healed for him. Her touch alone had been enough to soothe the pain.

"Sir?" Jacobs said. "What would you like us to do next?"

"We need shelter. The *Drigon* isn't much good for anything—not anymore."

"Can't we just stay here?" Temple asked.

"I doubt the power will hold up," Meredith piped in.

Temple glared at her. "What would you know about it, doctor?"

Dawson bristled. He didn't like the other man's tone. "Hanson, you and Timmons go check the power supply on the bridge."

"Yes, sir," Timmons responded, heading back out the doors.

"Meredith, how are they?"

She shook her head. "They aren't looking good. A RemLite can only do so much. The rest of my equipment is smashed and won't work without power anyhow. I'm surprised the replicator wasn't damaged, but the wall it's on seems intact."

Dawson shoved his hand through his hair and shook his head. "And we can't use the replicator to make more."

"No, but how I wish I could. The replicator can't reproduce complicated machinery. It only makes simple things like food and bandages, and that's only if there are sufficient elements in the tanks for it to use." She sighed. "Unfortunately, we won't get much out of it. With so much of the ship damaged or gone, the reserves are probably low."

"Do the best you can," he said with a nod. "That's all anyone can ask of you."

The med lab doors inched open as Timmons and Hanson returned and made their way into the room. "The power supply is failing, sir, due to a cracked core. I don't think staying here would be a good idea," Timmons reported.

Dawson nodded. "Very well, then. We look for an alternate place to set up base camp."

"I think we landed near the caverns that the landing party and surface scans discovered," Timmons confided.

Dawson nodded. "Those who are able-bodied collect everything of use and head for the caverns. We'll need food, blankets and anything else that's salvageable. After we get set up at the caves, Timmons and I will return to the ship to see if we can get the emergency beacon working. I think it's more important, considering the environment and cracked core, to get everyone to safety before checking the ship over." He sighed as he looked around at his surviving crew. "I'll need those of you who are able to carry them," he said, pointing to the critically injured. "Is this all that's left of us?"

"I'm afraid so, sir," the crewman said. He placed a bundle of coats on top of one of the tables.

"Only eleven out of forty people survived?"

"The hull had been breached in three sections, sir, before we ever left orbit. The mess hall was one of them. I know several men were in there for the evening meal."

Dawson's eyes closed. A wave of grief washed over him. So many lives lost and for what? McAllister's attempt at gaining ground for the Alliance? Well, damn the Alliance. It wasn't worth this. It never had been.

"Let's move out," he finally said. "Some of us will have to return later for more supplies."

"I can carry some," Meredith told him, stuffing things into a pack as she spoke.

"Anything you can manage will be a big help."

He filled a pack with the supplies that had been carried in as Timmons gathered up blankets to cover the wounded. They would need all the warmth they could get once they made camp, and there was no other way to carry them at the moment.

"Ready?" Dawson asked, moving his gaze over the small group. Everyone nodded. "Then let's head out. There's not much daylight left and, in these weather conditions, I don't know how long it'll take us to reach the caves."

* * * * *

He rose from the snow, slowly separating himself from the crystalline substance. The vibration echoing through the planet had finally subsided, but that hadn't deterred him any. He'd spent centuries alone here, and he knew this world well. Now on the brink of his departure someone else had dared to encroach on his domain.

The scent of smoke and death lingered in the air. He was close—very close. The broken and charred remains of the ship loomed up before him and anger welled up inside. Pure rage.

He picked up a fragment of the ship and slammed it against the snow-covered ground then threw it with all his might. This was his — his world. What made them think they could come here and disturb what was his?

Destroy, the voices whispered in his head. *Ours. Kill intruders.* The relentless voices and their words were hypnotic, leaving him little choice but to obey.

He snarled and growled. Yes, first remove the threat to that which he had claimed as his own then he'd seek out a new world on which to feed.

Blood and flesh were not needed to survive, but such a sweet treat they made. He slinked through the snow until he found the first body then he fed in order to sate the unrelenting voices so that he might have even a few moments of peace.

* * * * *

The wind howled and the storm blasted as Dawson led his ragtag team through a world of white. He glanced over at Meredith, thankful to her for her insight in the snowshoes she'd had the replicator create. He headed in the direction his pocket scanner told him shelter was located. The biting cold froze their exposed skin, but they moved on. They had to reach the caves before they froze to death.

When the caves finally loomed up, they picked up the pace, eager to reach shelter. Meredith's eyes moved from one cavern to the next then darted up to Dawson's tall figure at the lead. She stomped through the snow taking the longest strides her legs would allow.

"Dawson," she called out. The howl of the wind was loud and she nearly had to scream to be heard over it.

His gaze turned to her. "What?"

"I don't think these are caverns. Did the landing party even take a close look at them?"

"What makes you think that they aren't?" he asked, glancing back at the area in question. "They look like caves to me."

"I think they're some kind of houses. Crude ones, I agree, but houses nonetheless. The formations don't look natural to me," she pointed out.

Dawson returned his gaze to the shelter before them and nodded.

Meredith trudged on, and stepped inside the closest dwelling and dug into her pocket for a light. Snow covered the floor for a good distance inside, but the deeper she went into the structure, the less snow she found. The interior was a surprise.

Tattered pieces of faded, multicolored cloth hung from the ceiling, and other scraps lay against one wall, a makeshift bed, she presumed. A circle of stones sat in the center of the room, and a pile of sticks and logs rested against the wall by the entrance. How long had these items been there? And where had the inhabitants they belonged to gone?

She turned back to the entrance. "Dawson, in here. Bring the wounded in here," she called out, unaware that she kept calling him by his first name. She ran back to the stone circle. Delving into her pocket again, she pulled out a firestarter and in no time had a fire burning within the circle.

Warmth! Oh, it seemed an eternity since she'd last been warm. A sound behind her caused her to spin around. Dawson stood in the doorway staring down at her. A grin curved her lips upward.

"Need a little heat?" she asked.

Her face glowed in the light of the fire and her coat hood was down, allowing her hair to frame her face. She looked *so* enchanting, and just seeing her created the heat that he needed to see through this setback.

He stepped aside to allow the wounded to be placed near the fire. Meredith grabbed her bag and set to work examining the injured as he silently crept out. He had to get back to the *Drigon* and make sure the beacon was working properly in case no one had intercepted their distress call. The sooner help arrived, the sooner they could go home and he could throttle McAllister.

He paused at the entry, allowing his gaze to roam over their surroundings. A skeletal forest stood in the distance. Mountains circled the small plain on which they were located and snow and ice covered the ground for as far as the eye could see. This planet was dead. Why anyone would think they could put an agri-station here was beyond him — it was a wasteland.

Eyes stared at him as he stepped from the small abode. His gaze traveled over each of them. They had all seen better days, but at least they were able to move around. They all depended on him for their survival. He would not let them down.

"Timmons, you're with me. The rest of you, scatter out through the forest and find more wood. I have a feeling it'll only get colder before the rescue team arrives," he ordered, pointing toward the remnants of the forest behind the men. He started to walk away when he paused and turned back to his men. "On second thought, Hanson, you stay here and help Meredith if she needs it. The rest of you go search for wood. We'll be back as soon as we get the beacon operating."

He hated to leave Meredith, but the wounded needed her. An overwhelming need to protect her enveloped him. Dawson couldn't let his feelings for her interfere with his job. The situation they found themselves in wasn't easy for anyone, but what choice did he have? Three of those men were critically wounded, dying even, and she was the only one qualified to care for them. His crew was composed of good men. They would protect her just as he'd ordered, or they'd pay dearly.

That thought made him feel a little better, but something at the back of his mind continued to nag at him. Something didn't feel quite right, and until he figured out what that something was...

He had to stop being so negative. They would hopefully all get off this godforsaken planet alive despite the harsh environment. He'd show McAllister that he wasn't so easy to be rid of.

With that in mind, he walked across the snow and back to the *Drigon*, his baby. His heart ached at the loss of such a great ship. He'd planned to go back into the shipping business with her once he retired, but now that was a shattered dream. There just wasn't enough of her left to be salvageable.

"I'm sorry, sir," Timmons said at the look on the older man's face. "I know she meant a lot to you, but at least the Alliance will replace her."

Dawson nodded. "Yes, they will, but it won't be the same. She and I went way back. It'll take some getting used to. I had big plans for this old bird." He lovingly ran a hand over the icy hull.

"She was a fine ship, sir. I'm sure she'll make the Hall of Records."

Dawson laughed. A fine ship she was, but worthy of the Hall of Records? He doubted it, but it made no difference. The ship was the first one he had owned—all his. He had loved her and that was all that mattered to him.

"Let's find that beacon and get it working. Then we'll collect the bodies and store them away for when the rescue team gets here," he said as he moved into what remained of the bridge. He looked around at the damage and was surprised they had survived the crash at all.

"Sir, there are no life forms on the planet that could harm the bodies and with the temperatures being so low…" Timmons began.

"I said we'll collect and store the bodies. Would you want to be left lying around in the snow?" he asked.

Timmons looked embarrassed. "No, sir, I wouldn't."

"Then let's set to work so we can get back to the others," Dawson replied. The fires weren't the only thing he wanted to get back to, but he held his tongue.

"Yes, sir." Timmons grinned.

Chapter Five

ဢ

Meredith wiped the blood from the corner of Ferreti's mouth. He had internal injuries, and with nothing more than basics, she was helpless to do anything but sit back and watch him die. *At least he won't be in pain*, she thought as she administered another painkiller into his arm. She hated this part of the job. Her training was to help people. She hated feeling helpless, failing.

"Thank you," he rasped. His voice was so low that she had to lean forward to hear him.

She weakly smiled down at the dying man. "It's my pleasure. Now rest." She pressed a hand against his shoulder forcing him to lay back.

"Do you believe in angels, Dr. Carson?"

Her head nodded. "Yes, I do."

A weak smile met her answer. "You should, since you *are* one."

"I'm no angel, Ferreti. I'm just a woman with a job, and I'm sorry I can't be of more help to you." She smiled sadly and reached out her hand to slick back his hair from his forehead.

His hand slowly moved up to touch hers. "You've been more help than you'll ever know."

His grip on her hand loosened and he exhaled a final time. Meredith took a calming breath before she reached out and closed his eyes.

They were now down to ten. She looked over at the other wounded men. Their chances of survival were bleak but, then again, so were those of the remaining crewmembers.

She couldn't think that way. They would survive this. Dawson would make sure of it or die trying. A shiver ran down her spine at the thought. If anything happened to him, she didn't know what she'd do. Would she be able to live a life without Dawson in it? Whether they survived this harsh planet or not, the possibility of losing him stood before her.

She sighed and tears fell down her cheeks. Rising, she walked to the door. "Hanson, could you come in here please?"

"What's wrong, Dr. Carson?" he asked as he neared her.

"Ferreti. He's gone." She swallowed the lump in her throat. "We lost him. I want you to get a couple of the other men and move him to one of the other buildings."

Hanson nodded his head. "Yes, ma'am. Don't worry, Dr. Carson. We'll take care of it for you. Do you need anything else?"

"Not that I can think of."

"Oh, before I forget. I ran an analysis of the ice. If you need any water, it's safe to melt the ice and drink."

"Thank you, Hanson." She turned her attention to Santos and Regan. There was no way she was going to watch Hanson carry Ferreti's body out.

Hanson had just left when a scream of pure terror split the silence around them. Meredith jumped to her feet and rushed to the door. Outside, the snow swirled in a blinding pattern that made it impossible to see more than a few inches in front of her.

The sound had been too far away to have come from Hanson, but what of Dawson and the other men? Shivers ran down her spine and terror pierced her heart at the thought that something could have happened to Dawson. But they were alone on the planet, save for the men—what could possibly have happened that Dawson couldn't handle?

Another screech echoed across the snow-covered land and panic set in. That sound hadn't been human. It couldn't have been. Something else was out there, but how? She'd seen the reports herself. The BIOscan had found nothing, no signs of life, not even the tiniest bits of microscopic life.

Her heart pounded and her breath rushed out. She was terrified. Something was out there, an unknown entity powerful enough to mask its presence—and they were in its territory.

She closed her eyes, and her thoughts went to Dawson. He was strong and capable. She knew he'd return unharmed…he had to.

* * * * *

Dawson carefully moved through the debris littering the bridge floor, which had buckled on impact. The entire ship was smashed, stretched and twisted during their crash landing. Nothing was where it should have been, which made this job all the harder. He pulled his personal scanner out of his pocket and pressed in a series of commands that set it to searching for the ship's mobile analyzing unit. There was no way to know if the emergency beacon was functioning properly until he found that unit.

He looked over at Timmons. "Find anything over there yet?"

The other man shook his head. "No, sir, but things were shook up pretty bad during the landing."

"It's got to be here somewhere," Dawson muttered more to himself as his scanner began to beep. He tucked it back into his pocket and started tossing bits of wreckage out of the way until he reached a panel on the floor. Hooking his fingers in the depression designed for easy removal of the panel, he pulled it out and tossed it aside before he reached into the deep, dark compartment.

"Timmons, get over here and give me a hand," he ordered as he pulled the large silver case from its hiding place.

"Do you think it's still working, sir?" Timmons used his foot to slide more of the wreckage out of the way.

"It should be, son, but it never hurts to be certain." Dawson slid the case onto the spot Timmons had cleared and flipped it open. He pressed his thumb against the scanner and a screen unfolded from the case.

"Hello, Captain Lang. What are your orders?" the A.I.'s feminine voice asked.

"Analyze beacon output and functionality."

"Computing."

Dawson watched as lines of readout quickly scrolled across the screen.

"Analysis complete. Beacon functioning at one hundred percent, but not at the adequate frequency.

Atmospheric anomalies interfering with broadcast," the computer reported.

"Damn," he muttered under his breath. Dawson pulled his personal scanner back out of his pocket and set it down into the syncing cradle on the analyzer. "Computer, set up scanner to locate and recalibrate the beacon."

A beeping noise sounded. "Operation completed."

He picked up the scanner and activated it, then followed the blinking light on screen to the location of the beacon. "Here, Timmons. According to the scanner, it's under here." Dawson looked from where it should have been to where it was currently located. "That's more than twenty feet from where it originally was."

Timmons nodded. "I've got it, sir." He looked up at Dawson before going after the beacon. "It was a hard landing, sir."

"That is was."

Dawson watched as the younger man rummaged through the debris on the floor panels, which Timmons then deftly removed. Timmons laid down on the floor and reached down into the opening he'd created. "Got it, sir." He shifted to his knees as he pulled the small, black box from its hiding place.

Timmons looked up at him. "How do we get into it?"

Dawson shook his head. "Wasn't that a part of your basic training in academy?"

Timmons blushed. "Yes, sir. I just forgot under the circumstances."

"These types of circumstances are when you need to keep your head and your wits about you, son."

He watched as the younger man depressed the buttons on either side of the box and the lid slid open. Timmons moved back as Dawson approached the beacon, scanner in hand and ready to use.

He touched the security pad on the device first to identify himself as ship's captain to prevent the system from protecting itself. The jolt wouldn't kill him, but it sure would hurt like hell. It was set up as a safety measure to prevent someone from tampering with the emergency system, and though he understood the need for it, it sure did make his job at the moment a little trickier.

"Security parameters disengaged," a feminine voice reported.

"Prepare for link-up," Dawson ordered as he extended his personal scanner out in front of him.

A slender, metallic rod rose up from the beacon and inserted itself in the scanner's bottom side. The two devices clicked and beeped, then the rod retracted. "Synchronization complete."

"Run system analysis." Dawson slid his scanner back into his pocket as he awaited the results.

"New data assimilated. Now functioning at one hundred percent with maximum results. Broadcast now penetrating atmospheric anomalies without incident."

Dawson rocked back on his feet and let out a sigh of relief. He could have made the alterations manually, but it would have been a tricky situation. Shifting his gaze, he narrowed his eyes on the ship's main comms unit. "Think that thing is still functioning?"

Timmons shrugged. "We can try it, sir."

Dawson nodded. "You do that while I see if I can gather up any more supplies."

"Yes, sir."

Pulling out his pocket light, Dawson stepped into his quarters. He gathered what few blankets were on his bed and rolled them up for easier transport. In one of the bedside drawers, he located his spare pocketknife and slid it into his pants pocket for safekeeping. He went through his storage compartments and gathered anything he thought would be of use—extra shirts and socks, anything to help keep him and the crew warm.

"Sir, I think it's working. I sent out another distress call, but I'm not sure it's getting off the planet's surface."

"You did the best you could. Let's get out of here and see what else needs to be done and get back to camp. We'll carry back more supplies and maybe we'll get lucky enough to get someone to cook something for us."

"Sounds like a plan, sir," the younger man replied.

Dawson moved out of his room and started back out toward the corridor leading to the hull breech. He abruptly stopped midway. Something was amiss.

"Timmons, did you move the lieutenant's body?" he asked. He feared the crewman's answer.

"N-no, sir. I didn't," he stammered. "Are you certain he was dead, sir?"

"Timmons, I think I've seen enough dead bodies to know when one is stone-cold dead. Yes," he hissed. "I know he was dead. No pulse. No respiration. Dead."

"Okay, sir, I trust your judgment, but he didn't just walk off," Timmons pointed out. "And come to think of it, Casavont is missing too, sir."

"Shit! What the hell is going on here?" He paced the small space in the wrecked corridor. "We're not alone on this planet."

"But the BIOscan detected no signs of life, sir. There has to be another explanation."

Dawson shook his head. "Are we sure the BIOscan is always right? All survivors that we know of went with us, and if anyone else did survive, what purpose would there be in moving the body?"

"There is no purpose in moving the body. Not with no way off the planet." Timmons paused and looked around them. "There were no known life forms detected on this planet, sir, but—"

"But maybe there are unknown life forms on it. Damn it all to hell. We can't get a break, can we?"

"It doesn't appear so, sir, but if a life form was on this planet, the scanners would have found it. Wouldn't they? It is an ice planet."

"Something besides us is definitely on this planet, Timmons, whether the scanners showed it or not. And I have a feeling it's *not* friendly," Dawson remarked. "Come on, let's see about the other casualties and get the hell out of here. The sooner we get back to base camp, the better."

They began a search pattern that encompassed the entire debris field. Metal reflected the waning light of the sun, marring the pristine white snow.

The only evidence they found of the crash's casualties was where the snow had been stained red with blood. "What the hell?" Dawson muttered. "This isn't right. We need weapons and more supplies. Timmons, do you think the replicator in med lab might still be working?"

"It's possible, sir, but I doubt it'll have much power left. We probably depleted the supply earlier." He paused before adding, "Sir, it won't create weapons."

"I know it won't. Those crates outside the bridge, which were in the bulkhead, should have weapons in them. Let's check that first, then we'll make more supplies and get back to camp."

Dawson led the way back to the bridge and began breaking open the supply crates scattered about. "Bingo!" he shouted, having found what he was looking for. "Stun batons." He glanced over his shoulder at Timmons. "You find anything?"

"A couple laser pistols. Most of this stuff is severely damaged."

"Yeah, a lot of these are too." He unloaded what wasn't usable then moved the crate closer to Timmons. "Put what we can use in here then we'll go get what supplies we can, if we can, and get back to base."

"Here, sir," Timmons said, handing a laser pistol to Dawson. "Better safe than sorry."

Timmons stood with the crate in hand. Dawson nodded and led the way back toward the med lab. "Let's hope the replicator's got enough life left to give us a few more supplies."

"Yes, sir."

Dawson led the way into the med lab and set to work replicating food packets and backpacks in which to carry the items. He also made extra clothing and blankets to protect against the biting cold.

Timmons set to work making a sled out of parts of the broken tables and chairs while Dawson worked the replicator. He loaded the packs as Dawson waited on the device to do its job.

Dawson created as much as the replicator could manage before completely depleted of power and supplies. "Guess this will have to do." He rubbed his hand over the back of his neck. "Let's just hope the rescue team hurries up and arrives."

He helped load the sled before he grabbed a couple of the packs Timmons had loaded and slid them onto his shoulders. "Ready to go? I don't want to be caught in the dark with that thing, nor do I want to leave the camp unprotected."

"Yes, sir," Timmons replied as he finished securing ropes to the makeshift sled and stood. He handed one rope to Dawson. "This thing should slide easily over the snow. Hopefully it won't slow us down too much."

"It's just something we'll have to deal with." Dawson patted the pistol at his hip. "Let's just hope whatever's out there doesn't make an appearance."

Timmons nodded in agreement as Dawson set out back across the snow toward the crude abodes where they were currently camped. They trudged through the snow as fast as they could, especially carrying extra weight. As the minutes slowly dragged by, Dawson's mind spun numerous scenarios on what he might find once he returned to camp. He feared the worst, but prayed for the best. She would be fine, and so would the remainder of his crew. They had to be. He was responsible for them.

The sight of his men converging in front of the abode that housed Meredith stopped him dead in his tracks. Something was wrong, but what?

Taking a deep fortifying breath, he slowly moved forward. His heart pounded in his chest both from the trek through the snow to camp and from fear. If anything had happened to Meredith or any of his crew in his absence, he'd never forgive himself for failing them. He shouldn't have left them behind, but he'd done what he'd thought best at the time. *Fuck!* He was getting real tired that he seemed to have no choices since he had arrived at this hellhole.

"Dawson," her voice cried out as he stepped into the circle his men had formed.

A wave of relief washed over him at the sound of her voice. He turned his attention to her and nodded.

"What's going on here?" he asked. He tore his gaze from hers and looked at his men.

"Sir, maybe we should talk elsewhere," Temple said as his eyes darted toward Meredith then back over to Dawson.

"I am not some idiot who needs to be protected," she shot at Temple. "I'm a medical officer. Chief medical officer of the *Drigon*, in fact. I have a right to know what's going on."

Temple looked to Dawson for approval. Dawson smiled as he understood that his men recognized Meredith as his—his responsibility, his woman. When Dawson nodded his head, the explanations began. "Sir, we've had an unexpected casualty in your absence. I believe we have a murderer among us."

Dawson knew better and he suspected something worse. Nevertheless, nothing should be left to chance. In a survival situation, one never knew who could handle the pressure—or not.

Meredith shook her head. "As I keep trying to tell them, it wasn't a person."

"Sir, with all due respect, there's no way she can know that. She was inside with the wounded the entire time," Temple replied.

Dawson looked to Meredith who was red in the face, though he had no way to know if it was from anger or the cold. "What makes you think it wasn't human?" He had to know what she knew.

"I heard a scream, and it was unlike anything I'd ever heard before. No man could have made the sound." She shivered and ran her gloved hands up and down over her arms.

"Who's the victim?" he asked. "And why didn't you bring him back here?"

"Ainsley, sir. We were gathering wood as ordered when he screamed. By the time we reached him..." His words trailed off and his face paled. Again, Temple's eyes shifted to where Meredith stood. "There wasn't enough of him left to bring back, sir."

The words hit him like a fist in the gut. "Bowman! Temple!" he bellowed.

"Sir?" they both responded.

"You two are in security."

Bowman nodded. "Yes, sir."

"I need you to open that crate there and pass out the weapons. If anyone doesn't know how to use it, it's your job to make sure they learn." He turned to the rest of the crew and Meredith. "Temple, I want you to take me to the body. Jacobs, you're coming too."

"Show me where Ainsley is." He turned to Meredith. "Stay here."

"No." She moved forward. "I will *not* be ordered to stay like some dog. I'm coming with you. In case you have forgotten, this is a part of my job," she told him.

Dawson was at war with himself. She was chief medical officer, hell, she was currently the only medical officer at the moment. And she was right, her expertise would be needed, yet he knew how dangerous this could be. A part of him wanted to keep her in base camp where she'd be safe. On the other hand, if he took her with him, at least he could keep an eye on her. Reluctantly, he nodded. "Okay, you can come too."

He held his hand out to Bowman, who placed a pistol in his hand. "Can you shoot this?" he asked Meredith.

She nodded. "If I have to. Kaz insisted I learn before joining the crew."

There was that man's name again. He had no idea why, but every time she mentioned this mystery person, his blood boiled.

"Good, that makes me feel at least a little better about you going." Okay, so that was a lie, but she didn't have to know it. He handed her the gun, which looked unusually large in her small hand. She flashed him a weak smile and stuffed it into her pocket.

He nodded. "Okay, then let's go. Everyone else, stay here together. From now on, no one goes off alone. Understood?" He watched them all nod in acknowledgment. "Hanson, you and Bowman stay inside with the wounded," he ordered. He noticed the brief flash of pain that sparked in Meredith's eyes. "What's wrong, honey?" he asked, oblivious to the endearment he'd used.

"We lost Ferreti while you were gone, and the others aren't far behind him."

He placed a hand on her shoulder. "It's okay, Meredith. You've done all you can to save them," he reassured her.

"I know, but it still bothers me. I failed them, Dawson."

He tipped her chin up and smiled softly. "We'll discuss this later. Right now, we have more pressing matters to attend to. No one here, or anywhere else, holds you at fault for their deaths."

"Let's go," she said with grim determination. "I'm ready."

"Good. Temple, lead the way."

They slowly made their way toward the skeleton forest in the distance as the snow fell around them. The wind chilled them to the bone. Their hearts pounded in anticipation and fear of the unknown.

Temple led the way with Meredith behind him and Dawson and Jacobs behind her. Dawson kept Meredith in his line of sight at all times, whether she was aware of it or not. The thought of something happening to her did funny things to his insides and he tried to push his emotions to the back of his mind. His body, however, betrayed him and his thoughts. Even with them in danger and on his way to investigate a death, he was painfully aroused. *This is ridiculous.*

Their one time together had been exquisite, and his body longed for more. Now more than ever, he found himself wishing for time alone with her, next to one of those crackling fires back at camp. *Maybe...* He shook his head. This was *not* the time for such thoughts. He needed to keep his head on straight and his mind focused on the task at hand. His crew depended on him for their survival.

"We're almost there," Temple called out over the roar of the wind. He pointed toward a small group of bare trees in the distance.

Once they entered the skeleton forest, the wind wasn't so biting. The barren trees lent an eerie feel to their surroundings. The silence was deafening, the air around them bone-chilling, and the snow continued to fall heavily in the dimming light. Faint impressions from where the crew had trudged through the snow littered the ground, telling Dawson that it hadn't been long since his men had last been there.

"Where is he, Temple?" Dawson asked.

"Right over here, sir," the man replied as he rounded the trees.

All four froze when they came upon the spot. Not much was left of the man. If it hadn't been for the fact they already knew who it was, he wouldn't have been identifiable.

Blood splattered the snow, lending the whiteness eerie hues from pale pink to crimson red. It even dotted the ashen trunks of the trees. A large red circular pattern surrounded the remains, and all the visible prints looked to be human. But what human could cause such damage?

Meredith gasped and swallowed hard. From what the others had said, she'd expected a horrible scene, but this — this went beyond her imagination. She'd seen many gruesome sights during her medical training, yet this was just beyond her scope. What could have done this? And better yet, where was it?

She darted her gaze to the distant horizon. The sun had already sunk low in the sky. It would be dark soon, and they wouldn't be able to see well enough to investigate before long. Not to mention that the snow was covering up the evidence of the attack.

Desire to return to camp overwhelmed her. Fear left a bitter taste in her mouth and her heart pounded out of control. *You can do this, Mere, don't turn into a coward now.*

"Can you handle this, Meredith?" Dawson asked.

His blue gaze was piercing, watchful. She nodded. "Yes. I can." She would and she could and, if need be, she'd be sick later when there was no audience.

Meredith swallowed hard and lowered herself down beside the body. The snow crunched loudly in the silence as she knelt down beside the body. She did her best to ignore the icy chill of the wind, the lump in her throat and the rapid rhythm of her heart.

"There seems to be some sort of bite marks on the bones," she began, gently lifting one of the larger bones and turning it over in her gloved hands. "From the size of the marks, I'd guess it to be a fairly large creature, difficult to say more without any type of equipment."

"Anything else?"

She gazed around her at the blood splatter. "There's not enough blood here. Not nearly enough."

"Looks like a lot to me. It's even on the nearby trees," Dawson replied.

"There should be more blood. The human body contains several quarts of blood, much more than what's here. This is just a mere fraction. If I had to guess, I'd say whatever did this probably drank it or, for some reason, disposed of it." She dropped the bone in her hand and climbed back to her feet. "The entity that did this is very powerful. It ripped him to shreds. It stripped off his skin then went on to the fatty tissues and muscles until all that was left is what we see here. Have you ever tried to rip apart an animal with just your bare hands, your teeth?

Whatever it is, it's very powerful. That's all I know for certain."

She rubbed her gloved hands together, but the blood had already soaked in. "What now?"

"I'm going to find this thing. *You* are going back to camp. It's bad enough I allowed you to come out here, but I'll be damned if I let you go off on a monster hunt."

"Oh, no, Captain, you're wrong. You said so yourself at the camp, no one is to be left alone. I'm not leaving you out here by yourself, monster or not," she said through her teeth.

He grabbed her by the shoulders. "Look, Meredith. I'll be fine, and I won't be alone. Jacobs will be here."

"That's not enough. There were four of them, and look what happened." She motioned toward the remains.

"We'll be fine. We won't leave each other's sight. You can't go back by yourself. Temple will escort you, and then he and Hanson can come back and help me if it'll make you feel better. If I went back too, we both know that by the time we got back here the snow will have everything covered up. We can't afford to lose the time."

"I don't like this, Dawson. I don't like it at all. It's not any safer for you to be out here than it is for anyone else." She paced a small bit then paused to look up at him. "Just remember, I don't have any equipment besides a RemLite. I can't treat you or anyone else for hypothermia. I can't even do anything for our injured men except sit back and watch them die while pumping them full of painkillers. I won't do that with you. Do you hear me?"

"I'll be fine, Mere. Promise." He kissed her on the forehead. "Temple, accompany the doctor back to camp, then you and Hanson rejoin me. Jacobs and I will scout on ahead and see if we can find any tracks, any signs of what did this. Ours will be fresher, surely they'll still be visible when you get back."

Temple nodded. "Yes, sir."

"Hurry," Dawson repeated, pushing her into motion.

Meredith glanced back over her shoulder at him. She didn't like leaving him out here without more backup. "Be careful, Dawson."

* * * * *

Dawson watched her go with a troubled mind. He knew that making her return to camp was the right thing to do, though a part of him couldn't help but worry. The thing that stalked them could be anywhere. What if he'd just sent her into its path?

Reluctantly, he turned his attention away from Meredith's retreating back and focused on the mutilated body. Ainsley had been a quiet one, never causing any trouble. A real shame to lose someone so young to such a violent end.

"Any ideas on what caused this, sir?" Jacobs asked.

Dawson shook his head. "It's unlike anything I've ever seen." He looked around the body. "The better question is, where'd it come from? Do you see any tracks?"

He griped his pistol in his hand and circled around, watching the snow for any signs of tracks. Footprints littered the ground, but they were all human, belonging to his crew. He lifted his gaze to the treetops. Had it used the trees for travel? He didn't see anything up in the high branches, but that didn't mean it wasn't there, watching…waiting.

"The only tracks I see are from the rest of us who were out here with him. What can move through snow without leaving any signs?" Jacobs continued, pausing beside Dawson.

"Nothing that I know of." He glanced back up at the trees. "Could it have been in the trees?"

Jacobs shook his head. "There's nowhere for it to hide up there, sir. We'd have seen it. If it was big and strong enough to do this, I don't see how it could have hidden in bare limbs."

Dawson didn't want to admit it, but it was a rather unbelievable scenario for him too. "Go that way, Jacobs, and I'll go this way. We'll do a larger circle around the remains and see if we can find anything. Maybe it jumped—jumped a long distance to attack."

"Could be, sir."

They moved around the body in slow circles, making them larger with each pass. The last of the day's light was quickly fading away, and still they found no clues as to what had attacked.

"Sir, it's getting to hard to see."

"I was just thinking that myself. Let's head back to camp. Hopefully, we'll run into Hanson and Temple on the way back." He glanced back at the remains that were now liberally covered in snow. "I don't like the looks of this one bit."

"Me either, sir." Jacobs wrapped his arms around him and visibly shuddered.

A sudden gust of wind nearly toppled him over. He pulled the collar of his coat closer around himself and headed back toward camp with Jacobs following along behind. Tomorrow they'd come back out here and look around. Perhaps there'd be some signs of what they were dealing with. If not, they'd have to come up with a plan.

Chapter Six

ဆ

Hanson turned at the sound of someone entering the hut behind him. Dr. Carson stood in the doorway staring at where the men had been. She lifted her gaze to his. "Where's Santos?"

Hanson lowered his eyes and shook his head. "I'm sorry, ma'am. There wasn't anything you could have done. We thought it best to move him before you returned." He didn't tell her that they'd discovered Ferreti's body missing, nothing but blood left in its place.

Meredith nodded. "Yes, thank you." Her sadness reflected in her voice.

He watched her move to Regan's side and check him over. He felt bad for her but was at a loss as to what to say. Hopefully, this experience wouldn't leave deep emotional scars on her. She seemed so very young…

Hanson wanted to offer a word of comfort to her but thought better of it. He'd heard the rumors buzzing among the men. She belonged to the captain, and they'd do well to remember that.

He muttered his goodbyes, easing out of the building to leave her to her duties. He was so lost in thought that he nearly bumped into the subject of his musings. "Sir, sorry, sir!" he barked out, saluting the captain.

Dawson gave him an odd look and shook his head. The boy's head had obviously been in the clouds, but why? He saw nothing to be excited about, until he stepped into the building where Meredith sat with her coat off and her hair hanging down in a tangle of curls.

His heart slammed in his chest as jealousy gripped him, and he felt a strong urge to chase Hanson down and slug the man. If he took another step into the place, he'd ravish her right there in front of Regan, and that would never do. He narrowed his eyes at the picture before him as he realized something was amiss. Where was Santos?

Dawson turned and went back out the door. "Hanson, Timmons, watch over Regan. I need to have a private discussion with Meredith," he said. He caught Hanson by the arm as the younger man passed by. "What happened to Santos?"

"He died a little while ago. We moved him into one of the dwellings we aren't using so as not to bother Doctor Carson."

Dawson nodded his head. He was at a loss for words at the moment. Hanson moved inside with Dawson right behind him turning to where Meredith sat by the fire.

Without a word, he leaned over, took her by the wrist and pulled her to her feet. He wrapped a blanket around her shoulders and guided her out the door and into one of the other dwellings.

A fire crackled, reflecting an eerie orange glow into the darkness. The heat radiated outwards, encompassing them in its warm embrace, welcoming them inside.

Dawson guided her into the small structure, before turning to glare at his men who he could hear chuckling in the background. His glare silenced them as they disappeared inside the other huts where fires burned. He jerked the drape hanging over the door closed. Then he turned his attention back to Meredith.

She had spread a blanket across the floor near the fire and was sitting in the center of it running her fingers through her hair like a comb. Did she have any idea how beautiful she was? How badly he needed her at that moment?

Slowly he removed his outer gear then moved to her side and knelt down on the blanket. She looked up at him — her eyes full of emotion, causing his heart to contract painfully. This woman had the ability to stir him up and make him feel things he had never felt before, all with a single glance. Why had it taken him three months to finally admit that?

"I shouldn't have come," she whispered.

"What? Why would you say that?"

"Kaz didn't want me to come. He encouraged me to take technology classes and the other sciences in hopes I'd find a job on the home world. But I wanted to be in space, to visit other planets." She sighed. "That's why I went into the medical field. I saw it as my way out, but it wasn't. I don't think I'm cut out for this job, Dawson."

He brushed a stray lock of hair from her cheek and tucked it behind her ear. "For what it's worth, I'm glad you're here, Meredith. I mean, you know I wish none of us were here, stuck on this planet, but I'm glad you were onboard ship. You're a damn fine doctor and a beautiful woman. It does an old man good to see such a pretty, smiling face in the last few months of his career."

"You are *not* old," she chastised. She looked at his face, taking in each and every new worry line, tracing them with her fingertip. She noted the faint feathering of gray at his temple, but it did nothing to detract from his striking good looks. Meredith traced her fingers over his

91

features lovingly, a whisper of a butterfly's kiss tracing against his skin. "How old are you, Dawson?"

"Older than you are, sweetness," he replied. One large hand reached up to capture hers, pulling it away from his face. "I'm thirty-eight, and you don't look a day past eighteen."

Meredith laughed and shook her head. "I'm a doctor, remember? Medical school takes time, you know. You're not much older than I am." Her eyes sparkled up at him. "I'll be twenty-seven in…" she began and her smile faded. "Well, today, now that I think about it."

"And you didn't tell anyone?"

"You *are* the captain," she pointed out. "You have access to the files of every crew member. Besides, with these circumstances, it's no big deal."

"What a way to spend a birthday. Stuck on an isolated, supposedly lifeless planet with a creature that's slowly picking off the crew one by one," he muttered.

When Meredith shivered at his description, he regretted the words. "Oh, baby. I'm sorry. I shouldn't have said that."

She shrugged. "It's the truth. We both know it. I knew something was going on, but I thought the planet was uninhabited."

"I'm afraid the findings were wrong. Something is definitely out there." He refused to tell her everything, especially after her reaction to Ainsley. "Are you okay?"

"I'm fine, Dawson, really," she replied with more conviction than she felt.

He lowered his head to hers and met her gaze. "There's nothing wrong with being scared. Only a fool wouldn't be. But you, my lady, are a puzzle, one I intend to figure out. You're such a mix—brave, yet fragile."

"Careful I don't break." A soft moan escaped her lips when he gently kissed them.

She played at the buttons of his shirt and felt her body finally come alive again. The touch of his lips pressed firmly to hers made her feel weak at the knees. Her body ached to join with his, to feel his hard cock sliding into her tight sheath. She needed him so much more than she had ever dreamed possible. The combination of fear and passion was a powerful aphrodisiac.

"So sweet," he breathed against her lips. "So soft."

She tugged his shirt free and ran her hands over his smooth skin, enjoying the feel of his taut muscles. Her nails lightly raked down his back, and she smiled when he stiffened against her.

"Where are you from, Dawson? Originally?" she questioned when he lifted his head to gaze down at her.

"Texas. Why?"

"Mm, my very own space cowboy."

"Like that, do you?" he chuckled.

"Uh-huh, sure do. I can just picture you with a cowboy hat on, sitting at the *Drigon*'s controls."

His smile waned at her words.

"I'm so sorry, Dawson. I didn't mean to… I mean… God, I'm just so sorry."

"No, it's okay. You meant well. It's all right. Maybe some of her is salvageable."

"I hope so, Dawson. I truly do." Her hand reached out to caress his cheek. "You look so tired."

"More than you know. Why don't you come back over here and help me to relax?" He stood and slipped out of his jeans, then sat back on the blanket.

"Just what did you have in mind for that, Captain?" She knelt down and tugged his shirt over his head, smoothing her hands over the firm muscles before her, kissed him softly, then moved her hands up to his shoulders. Her palms kneaded his flesh, easing the tension and strain. After a few minutes, she ran her fingers down his stomach, allowing her nails to gently scrape against his skin.

Dawson shivered, squeezing his eyes shut. It felt so good to have her hands on him, to feel her soft touch gliding over his taut muscles. He groaned in surprised pleasure when he felt her hand snake its way down to take his cock firmly in hand. Her fingers played up and down, teasing him until he was full and hard, and then—she slid down. Her tongue swirled around his belly button and he couldn't resist raising his hips. The things she did to his body—his soul—made him feel more alive than he could ever remember feeling.

"You like that?" she murmured, her voice tickling his skin.

"Silly question, especially when you already know the answer," he replied through his teeth.

She laughed and withdrew from him. Standing, she moved around to stand in front of him, gazing into his eyes.

"My turn," she said with a smile.

Meredith pulled up her shirt then quickly lowered it back down. She taunted him with little glimpses of her breasts, enjoying his glittery stare. The cool air around them warred with the heat from the fire against her skin, causing chill bumps to form all over her body.

She pulled the shirt over her head, shaking her hair loose. Reaching up, she cupped her breasts in her palms, twisted her aching nipples between her fingertips, and then slid her hands down over her abdomen, to the fastening of her pants. Slowly, she undid it, peeled the fabric back and pushed it down her legs after she removed her boots and socks. The material pooled around her ankles as she stepped out of it and jumped into his lap.

"Since it's your turn, what would you like?" His lips moved over the pulse point at her throat, his tongue swirled over her heated skin.

She sucked in her breath as his touch played havoc on her senses. Her skin felt flushed, tension filled every muscle and a pleasant ache—a longing—washed over her in every place where their skin touched. He made it hard for her to think, much less speak.

"I...want...you," she gasped.

He slid his hands up over her torso, capturing her breasts in his large, calloused palms. His fingers gently pinched her nipples, before they glided lower to tease at the soft curls of her cleft.

"Want me where?" He nipped at her jawline with his teeth, teased the corners of her mouth with his tongue.

"Inside me." She whimpered when his finger delved into her heat.

"You feel so good, so hot, so juicy...you want me, Mere?"

She found herself screaming desperately, "Yes!"

He grabbed her hips with his hands, lifted her off his lap and slowly lowered her back down over his long cock.

She braced her hands on his shoulders, met his gaze as a small smile graced her lips. Slowly, she lifted herself up until only the tip of his erection remained within her before she slowly lowered herself back down. His face looked tense as she continued her gradual descent. She could feel the quiver of his arms as he strained to keep a hold on his control. Over and over, she tortured him with her movements. Withdrawing from him, only to slowly return to where she had been.

"I...need...more," he ground out between clenched teeth.

"Hmm, like this?" she asked in a husky whisper. She lifted herself up, slowly, once more then slammed down against him.

He moaned as she quickly repeated the action. Slow and torturous at first, then faster and harder at the end.

"Honey, wait," he breathed.

"What?" she asked, poised over him ready to dip down against him again.

"I think I need to change position," he laughed. "These joints can only take sitting here like this for so long."

She giggled and climbed off him. "You poor old thing. So now what?" she asked, hands on her hips.

"This," he said, grabbing her by the hand. He pulled her back down into his arms, and rolled over, pinning her beneath him and entered her again in one plunge. "My turn again," he smiled.

Meredith's head went back, her eyes closed and she gasped as he drilled into her. She loved feeling filled to overflowing. He moved over her and hit the sweet spot that sent electric shocks washing over her body in waves of unbelievable pleasure. Her body writhed beneath the heavy weight of his. She pushed her hips up, meeting his downward thrusts. Sliding her hands up his back, she ran her fingers through his hair, pulling his mouth down to hers.

Dawson kissed her with every ounce of his fiery need behind it. His body rocked back and forth over her. Each movement grew in speed and strength as he strove for fulfillment. He slammed in and out then held himself back until he felt her pussy contracting over him, gripping him, milking him of all he had.

Seconds later, Dawson followed her lead. His body stiffened above hers and his seed exploded into her pussy. He thrust slowly into her one last time, groaned and collapsed on top of her. He lifted his head and smiled down at her.

A realization crept into his mind as he stared down into her sparkling green eyes. He wanted to tell her that he loved her, but how would she react? She hadn't given him any indication that she felt the same, other than giving her body to him. Did that mean she loved him? She seemed to fall in headfirst, just as he did.

He rolled off her, pulling her along with him as he turned onto his side. "I could stay here like this forever."

"So could I, but we might get cold. The fire is dying."

He lifted his head to look at the dwindling fire. "So it is," he sighed. "You stay put, I'll add some wood."

"I need to check on Regan. He's the only one left," she said, pulling her shirt back over her head.

"Okay, baby. I'll walk you back." He began pulling on his own clothes, but his eyes kept darting to her slender form.

* * * * *

Dawson stood watching Meredith work from the door. His heart panged as he watched her hands slide over Regan's skin. He was so addicted to her that he found himself envious of the other man's injuries, and barely managed to stop himself before he charged in like some raging bull and jerked her away from her work.

Don't be stupid, Lang. He ran an unsteady hand through his hair. *You just had the most amazing sex with her not even an hour ago.* But even that thought was not enough to curtail the feelings of jealousy and possessiveness when it came to her. It was hell feeling this insecure. In the past, he had always known what to do, always known where he stood. What was the matter with him and what the hell did he know about women?

He abruptly turned away from the pair before him. Grabbing up a burning log from the fire to use as a torch, he walked through the snow toward the forest of dead, leafless trees without really seeing where he was going. If he didn't do something constructive with his time instead of watching Meredith work, he'd go crazy and possibly do something he'd later regret. Wanting her and this inactivity — waiting to see when the creature would strike next — was playing havoc with his temper.

The temperature dropped with each step he took. The snow fell even harder, covering his tracks in an icy white blanket. Common sense told him he should turn back while he could still find his way, but some vague hunch kept propelling him forward. He'd ordered everyone to stay together, yet he was out here alone in the darkness. Something out there beckoned to him, called his name — nothing more than a whisper in the wind — something was pulling him forward.

Only minutes later, he found he'd wandered much farther away from camp than he'd intended. The spot where Ainsley's remains had been found was far behind him, and still he trudged on.

A feeling of unease washed over him. He was no longer alone, but he couldn't see anyone in the ring of light cast by the torch.

Then he spotted her.

She had appeared as if from thin air, her figure slender and curved in all the right places. But she was unlike any woman he'd ever seen before. *My God, she's made completely of ice.* Long hair flowed down her back in waves, and her translucent body reflected the yellow-orange glow of the fire.

Her lips were moving, saying something, only he couldn't understand her words.

He moved closer, trying to hear the words she spoke, but all he heard was the faint whisper of the wind. For each step forward he took, she took a hasty step back. An arctic wind gusted, whipping across his face causing him to blink, and she was gone…vanished from sight.

Who was this strange woman? And why had she appeared to be made of the finest glass or the coldest ice? He didn't know, but he had every intention of finding out.

He remembered seeing glaciers in the distance during the day. They had to hold the key to this mystery. He headed that way—the way she'd been moving—as the darkness surrounded him and the snow fell.

The journey was long and difficult in darkness, but he didn't let it slow him down. The darker it grew, the colder it got. The biting cold wind whipped across the barren land and pushed at his back, urging him forward into an unseen, unknown force.

The cavern was blacker than pitch, but he felt compelled to enter. His foot was but a step away from crossing the threshold when voices in the distance broke through the spell he seemed to be under. The shouts grew louder with each passing second and he turned his attention to them.

As he moved forward to meet his men, a loud roar rumbled forth from the cavern behind him. Whatever was hidden in there was apparently pissed because he hadn't fallen into its trap.

The ground shifted beneath their feet. In the dim orange glow of the torches, they could see the snow rising as though something moved beneath the surface.

Dawson's eyes widened. "Where's Meredith?"

"We left her back at camp with the fires and Bowman. Regan couldn't be moved," Hanson explained.

"My God, it's gone after her," Dawson choked out. He set out at a dead run heading back to camp, oblivious to whether or not his men followed. He had to make it in time. He had to. This time, he couldn't fail.

* * * * *

Regan's breath came in gasps, his eyes had rolled back in his head and his body shook and trembled with fever. He was dying, and Meredith was helpless to do anything for him.

"I'm so sorry," she whispered. With a trembling hand, she wiped his brow and tucked the blankets closer around him.

As he drew in his last breath, tears gently rolled down her cheeks. She wanted to go home. This entire assignment had been nothing but a series of disasters, one after another.

A sound behind her caused her to turn her head and glance over her shoulder. "Bowman, is that you?" she asked, thinking the security man was trying to quietly check in on her.

At first, nothing was there. Then suddenly, she was no longer alone. A shadowy figure stood in the doorway.

"Bowman, this isn't funny." And it wasn't. If the crewman was playing tricks on her, it was downright low and dirty.

Panic swelled up inside her as she watched the figure sway back and forth, before moving into the circle of light cast by the fire. Reflections of orange and yellow flames danced along its tall form as water dripped and pooled at its feet.

Meredith leaned away, a hand to her mouth. She bit into the back of her hand, holding back the screams that threatened to rip from her throat.

What was this creature who looked so much like a man but appeared to be made completely of ice?

It moved closer. Reached for her. Stared at her with glowing red eyes. A clawed hand gripped her arm and she struggled to break free. Nails raked her arm as she threw herself forward, landing on her stomach, causing her hand to knock one of the logs free of the fire.

In an instant of pure panic, she grasped the burning log and quickly spun onto her back. Her arm flew out, dragging the log in a wide arc and hit the creature in the face with it.

The creature screamed in pain, agony and fury. It tried to move closer, but Meredith once again thrust the burning log in front of her, causing it to fall back. As it disappeared out the door in a blur of movement, she screamed with every ounce of fear inside her pushing the bloodcurdling sound from her lungs.

Bowman rushed in the door. "What happened, Dr. Carson? Are you all right?"

She shook her head as her entire body shook uncontrollably.

"You're bleeding," he said, dropping to his knees beside her. He rifled through her bags and dug out a bandage, which he wrapped around her wounded arm. "How'd this happen?"

"Monster," she whispered, never taking her eyes from the door.

Bowman jumped to his feet and moved to the door, poking his head out before turning back to her. "There's nothing out there."

Meredith inched as close to the fire as she dared. It'd been afraid of the fire—fire was safe. With a new log, she broke the circle of stones containing the fire, spreading it to cover a wider area. If it wanted back in the hut, it would have to walk through the flames to get her.

Pulling her legs up, she rested her chin on her knees and began to rock. The tears began raining down as she tried not to think of the monster outside and the corpse inside with her.

"Dr. Carson, ma'am, please don't cry." Bowman knelt beside her, but Meredith paid him no mind.

Meredith nodded her head, though she wasn't exactly sure what he was saying. Terror had a firm hold on her and wouldn't let go. All she could think about was staying close to the fire where it'd be safe, and pray that that thing didn't come back.

Chapter Seven

෴

A loud roar, followed shortly by a scream, rang out and Dawson felt his heart stop. He was too late. It had already reached her, and he was too far away to be of any help.

A renewed burst of speed sent his legs moving as fast as they could carry him. Adrenaline-rich blood pumped through his veins. The creature may already be there, but he would arrive in time to prevent Meredith from becoming its latest victim. The thought kept him running.

He slammed into the doorframe, unable to stop his forward momentum, only to find a roaring fire blocking his path and Bowman pacing the floor. Meredith sat just on the other side of the flames, rocking back and forth with blood soaking through a bandage on her arm.

"Bowman, what happened?"

The other man shook his head. "I dunno, sir. I stepped away from the door for just a few minutes to, umm—" he glanced at Meredith then back at the captain "—relieve myself when I heard the doctor scream. I came as fast as I could, but she was already going into shock and Regan had died."

Dawson nodded as he tried to assess everything the man had said. He leapt across the fire and dropped down beside her, before shooing Bowman out of the hut. At first, she didn't appear to see him. He feared that if he spoke, she would snap. Gently, he brushed the hair back from her face and she jumped away from his hand.

Quickly, he moved his hand back as she jerked back and raised her fist. He watched the emotions playing across her face. Wide-eyed shock was the first thing that registered then fear and, finally, recognition.

She fell into his arms, mumbling something he couldn't understand. Meredith wrapped her arms around his chest and buried her face in his neck.

Dawson ran a hand down the length of her tangled hair. "Oh, baby. I'm sorry. I'm so, so sorry. I shouldn't have left you alone here. Had I known it would come after you, believe me, you never would have been left vulnerable," he said quietly. His chin rested on top of her head and he rocked her comfortingly while she cried.

After a short while, when her sobs began to lessen, he leaned her back to look into her eyes. "Honey, we have to do something about that wound. We can't have our number one medic bleeding to death on us, can we?" He leaned over and reached into her pocket where she kept the RemLite. "Why didn't you use this on yourself?"

She smiled weakly and shook her head. "I don't know. Never occurred to me. I just wanted to stay close to the fire." She drew in a deep breath and glanced at him. "I'm so scared, Dawson."

"It's okay, baby. I'm here now."

"Do you know how to work the RemLite? It's the only instrument I have left. It should take care of the wounds without leaving a scar."

He could have laughed at that. She was clearly scared out of her wits, yet she was concerned about scarring. "I can do it, if you talk me through it." He knew how to use it, but keeping her busy was the best therapy right now. "Let me take care of Regan first, though. That's got to be making you uncomfortable." He stood and stamped out the fire from the path to the door. "Timmons, get in here!"

"Thank you," she murmured.

Timmons appeared in the door. "I need you and Bowman to take care of Regan," he ordered. "Then seek shelter in one of the other dwellings while I tend the doctor's wounds."

"Yes, sir," they both responded, moving to the task given them.

Dawson returned his attention to Meredith. "We need to get your shirt off, and I didn't think you'd like an audience."

"Thank you," she murmured softly.

"Okay, how do I work this thing?"

"The button on the side turns it on, but first hold it over the wound. A quick scan over each mark will stop the bleeding then go back slowly for a more detailed repair. Can you do it?"

He nodded his head. "Yeah, I think so."

Dawson helped her ease out of her shirt then held the RemLite up over the first of the wounds and clicked the button. A bright blue light began to emanate from the tip as Dawson passed it over the wound, stopping the bleeding.

He repeated the procedure with each of the five marks then went back to the first to begin the painstaking process of a thorough repair.

"There," he said. "All done."

Meredith moved her arm, eyeing him warily. "Not bad, for a space cowboy." A small smile played at the corners of her mouth.

He gave her a grin. "I try. Does it feel better?"

She nodded. "Much. Thank you."

He brushed his fingers along her newly repaired skin, testing his own work, and she shivered beneath his touch.

"Care to tell me what happened?" he asked as he continued to rub his fingertips over her arm.

"I thought maybe Bowman was checking up on me, but when I turned, it wasn't anyone I recognized. When it got closer and the fire lit it up, it was the strangest thing." She took a deep breath. "He looked like he was made completely of ice. What was it?"

Dawson shook his head. "I don't know, but I saw it too. I think it can change its shape."

"A shape-shifter? It's not like anything on record."

"I don't know what to make of it either." He tapped his fingers against his leg. "I wish help would hurry up and get here. I want off this planet."

"You and me both. Its eyes were bright red and seemed to glow brighter and brighter as it got closer."

"How'd you get away from it?"

"The fire. I picked up a log from the fire and swung it at its head. It roared and disappeared." She shivered.

Dawson pulled her into his arms and rubbed her back. "I'll keep you safe, Meredith. I promise you that."

She lifted her gaze to his—desire sparked between them. He played in her hair with his fingers, and she closed her eyes as she sighed.

Dawson moved his hand beneath her chin and tilted her head back to look into her green eyes. He kissed the tip of her nose. "I'm going to love you, Meredith. Think you can handle that?"

She nodded her head. "Oh, yes," she breathed. "I think I can."

"Good." He smiled down at her, running his hands down along the length of her arms. She was so small, so fragile at the moment that his heart ached to keep her safe and protect her from all things that could harm her. He needed to celebrate that she was alive and safe.

He slid his hands over her shoulders and brushed his fingers across the tops of her breasts. Slowly, he removed her shoes along with the rest of her clothes from her creamy skin.

"So beautiful, baby. Why it took me so long to realize that, I'll never know."

"Dawson, don't. It doesn't matter, does it? We're together now, aren't we?"

Dawson nodded. "Yes, we are. This is going to be slow and sweet. I plan to savor each and every inch of you. Sound okay to you?"

"Sounds perfect," she whispered.

He smiled. "Show me what you like, Meredith." He kissed her cheek, massaged the back of her neck. "Anything, baby. Anything at all."

She took his hands in hers and guided them to her bare breasts. He held their soft weight in his palms, massaging them carefully like he thought she wanted him to do.

He lifted his gaze to hers when she moaned. She surprised him by squeezing his fingers, tightening their grip on her nipples.

"Like that, do you?"

She nodded her head. "Very much," she sighed. She moved her hands up into his hair, pulling him closer.

He gently pushed her onto her back, laying her down on a blanket by the fire. He moved down her abdomen, kissed her stomach and licked a trail around her belly button. Dawson then blew softly across the slightly damp skin.

Pushing her legs apart, he lay down between them and ran his tongue between her wet folds. Dawson delicately spread her open with his hands, running a finger over her clit then twirled circles around it. He pushed his tongue through her opening, delving inside to taste her sweet juices. Inhaling deeply, he breathed in her musky scent.

"You smell so good. All salt and spice," he murmured.

He suckled her clit, nipping at it with his teeth, causing her to cry out in pleasure.

Meredith writhed beneath him, moving her hips each time he stroked her with his tongue. She tangled her hands in his hair, gasping for breath. Intense jolts of pleasure-pain shot through her each time he nipped at her sensitive nub. He dipped his tongue deeper into her opening and she quivered in response. She tugged at his hair, trying to pull him up to her. She wanted to feel his hard cock where his tongue savored and teased. She needed to be filled by him.

"Now, Dawson, I need you now."

He again parted her folds with his hands and blew air across her heated skin. She shivered under the cool feel of his breath and squirmed in an attempt to entice him to do more.

"Slow down, sweetheart. We've got time."

She shook her head. "No. I need you now. Want you to fill me. Please, Dawson, please." Her body was alive with feeling, each touch of his skin sent shocks chasing through her. If she didn't get him soon, she was sure she'd die of need.

"I'll make it well worth the wait, sweetheart, I promise you."

"I can't wa—" she gasped, unable to finish speaking when he placed his hot lips on her and sucked her clit directly once more.

She tensed and arched beneath the hot kisses he trailed up her body until he joined his lips with hers.

Meredith loved the feel of the weight of his body. She loved the way his hands played across her skin, yet she needed—wanted—more. Slipping her hands between them, she pushed upward against his chest. As he rose up, she shoved him hard, toppling him over. She moved over him and stared down into his face.

He blinked his big blue eyes, as if shocked by her actions. Meredith smiled as she lowered herself, rubbing her breasts against his hairy chest. She sucked his earlobe into her mouth, nipping it with her teeth. He moaned, and she moved her hips down, teasing and caressing his hard cock with her folds.

She slid back and forth over him leaving a wet trail, swirled her tongue across his skin, nipped at him with her teeth. Being in control gave her a sense of power such as she'd never known before, and she found that she liked it very much.

She ran her hands up into his hair, lifted herself up so he could suckle her breasts in turn. A sigh escaped her lips and her body rocked with a harder rhythm.

He rolled and entered her in one smooth stroke, filling her completely. He pumped, stretching her with each plunge of his hard cock into her pussy. She felt her juices flowing, surrounding him and welcoming him into her heated depths.

She raised her hips, her legs wrapped around him. His balls slapped against her ass with each thrust of his hips, and she arched her back, enjoying the rough abrasiveness of his chest sliding against her nipples.

Meredith grabbed his ass, pulling him closer, deeper. She tightened her legs around his hips, digging her ankles into the backs of his thighs to encourage him to speed up his thrusts. Her breath rushed out each time his hips slammed into hers. She bit his shoulder, clawed his back and moaned in response to his body's movement.

Her pussy tightened with each stroke, grasping him and refusing to let go. The increasing tension snapped and she threw her head back, screaming out her release, not caring if anyone heard her.

She heard him groan as he increased the speed and rhythm of his movements. He roared as his cock throbbed and spurted while her body continued to spasm and milk him. Seconds later, he collapsed on top of her, gasping for breath.

Meredith reached up and smoothed the hair back from his face. She kissed his cheek and hugged him close. "You're such a wonderful lover."

"As you are, baby," he smiled down at her. "I don't know about you, but I'm exhausted." Dawson rolled off her, pulled her into his arms and let out a deep sigh of satisfaction.

"Yeah, I know the feeling."

He lifted his head and peered out at her from beneath his arm. "What are you talking about? I did most of the work."

Meredith laughed and stared at him. She picked up a wadded-up piece of material and tossed it at his head. "Yeah, right. I was right there with you step for step."

He pulled her close and kissed her. "I know *that* was my pleasure."

She shook her head. "You really are something."

"Is that a complaint?"

"No, never."

He leaned down and kissed her, a loud smacking sound that battled with the crackling fire for dominance in the room. "You stay put. I'm going to tend to the fire. I'll be right back."

"Thought you were exhausted?"

"Exhausted, yes, but not so much that I want to freeze."

"Oh, okay, but don't take too long. I might miss you," she murmured in return, a seductive smile on her face.

"I won't be gone that long." He winked and tugged on his jeans to tend the fire.

Meredith pouted. "No fair, you covered up."

He gave her a lopsided grin. "Darlin', it's not wise for a man to mess with a fire with his pride hanging out. Wouldn't be a pretty picture at all." He piled more wood onto the fire. "Ever wonder where the phrase 'chestnuts roasting on an open fire' came from?"

"Now *that* would be a shame," she smirked.

"Laugh it up while you can, but if I hadn't dressed, you may be babying me and going without sex. Can't have sex with crispy equipment," he told her in as serious a tone as he could muster. He tried to look stern as he gazed at her, but failed miserably. He would do anything in the world to see a smile on her face, to hear her laugh—anything.

She patted the blanket next to her. "Why don't you come back over here and let me kiss it and make it better?"

He raised an eyebrow at her as he moved closer to the door. He reached outside, plucked a piece of ice and laid it down. Good thing he had paid at least some attention to all the reports on the planet. The ice was safe for consumption, which would be needed if they were stranded for too long.

When he returned to her side, he reached and grabbed one of the strips of cloth from one of the other pallets.

"What are you doing?"

"Do you trust me?"

She swallowed. "I guess that depends on what you're planning to do."

He put a finger to her lips to silence her questions. "Trust me."

As she stared up at him in confusion, he moved her hands up over her head. She felt the fabric wrapping around her wrists and tried to pull her hands free, but his larger ones prevented the movement.

Dawson paused and gazed into her eyes. "Meredith, baby, we've done this before. I won't hurt you. If you really don't like it, just say so and I'll cut you loose...I promise."

She hesitated, but stopped struggling. He finished tying off the material, sliding his hands down her arms and over her breasts. He rubbed the piece of ice over her nipples, causing them to harden in pleasure and pain.

He moved the ice over her heated skin, leaving a trail of icy droplets behind. Leaning forward, he lapped up the cool liquid with his tongue, savoring the water as it mingled with her taste. His teeth nipped at her nipple as he ran the ice around the other one, causing it to harden.

"What do you want?" he murmured, his husky voice tickling her skin.

His hand holding the ice slid down her body, pressing the ice to the hard nub of her clit. Her body jerked as he slowly slid it between her hot folds.

"What do you want?" he asked again.

"You," she rasped out.

His slightly shaggy head shook. "That's not it. What do you truly want?" He ran the ice between her folds again, teasing it in and out of her opening. Dawson circled her nipples with his tongue then nipped at them with his teeth once more. He drew in a breath and blew it out slowly over her moist skin. "Say it," he murmured. "Tell me what you want me to do."

She tried to reach for him, but the ties at her wrists wouldn't let her do anything more than touch him when what she really wanted was to wrap her arms and her entire being around him. Her body throbbed beneath his touch, tempted him to take what was his. Meredith whimpered and her body shook when he pushed the ice into her pussy and withdrew it again.

"Fuck me! Now!" she yelled on a rush of breath.

A wicked smile curved his lips up at the corners. "My pleasure." He stood and helped her to her feet.

"Can you stand?"

She nodded as he helped her to her feet and led her to the wall. She faced it and pressed her bound hands against the smooth, cool stone, palms down to support her weight.

Dawson removed his pants, moved up behind her and spread her legs farther apart. His hands dug into her hips and she ground her ass against his cock. He pulled her back, seating himself fully in one stroke.

This time wasn't like the others. Instead of taking his time with her and trying to be gentle, he went fast and hard. This time his actions were driven by primal needs and desires.

His hips rammed against her ass, pushed his cock as far into her sheath as he could go. His heavy balls slapped against her pussy, building the pressure within her womb with each forward thrust. Leaning forward, he ran his tongue over her perspiration-covered back as he continued to pound within her heat. His hands gripped her hips until the knuckles went white when he felt her body contract around his. His sticky seed erupted into her, and he grunted as he continued to thrust into her until he could move no more.

Grabbing her around the waist, he slid his cock from her pussy and pulled her back down onto the blanket with him. He cradled her trembling form to him, stroking her side, kissing her hair.

"You okay?" he asked against her ear. "I didn't hurt you, did I?"

When she didn't answer, he pulled her closer. The sounds of her steady breathing greeted him. Reaching over to where his jeans lay, he dug in his pocket for his knife and cut the fabric from her wrists.

Dawson moved his gaze over the length of her exquisite body. As bad as he hated the idea of covering it up, he needed to at least get a shirt back on her to help keep her warm. The door only had a blanket hanging in front of it to keep the cold out, and the weather conditions outside were bitingly cold.

He dug in a pack for a fresh shirt and managed to get her into it, then pulled the blankets up tightly around her. He grabbed a shirt for himself and pulled it on before he turned his attention to the fire. Since he had no way of knowing how long they'd sleep, he wanted to make sure it had enough of wood on it to keep it burning for a while longer.

Snuggling close, Dawson hoped he would join her in sleep, if only he could get his still-hard body to relax, and not think about the danger that was out there.

Chapter Eight

෧

Meredith stood in the doorway staring out across the distance. The sun beat down on her and the green grass at her feet. Slowly, she moved out into its warmth, reveling in the feel of it heating her skin. The soft, lush grass tickled her bare feet as she moved out a few yards from the cluster of huts in the village.

A gentle breeze carried the sweet scent of wildflowers to tempt her senses. She let her head fall back and stretched her arms out, spinning in circles with her skirt flying out around her legs.

The village sat in the center of an alcove surrounded on three sides by tall, majestic-looking mountains and bordered by a lake on the fourth. The roar of the waterfalls could be heard in the distance as the water cascaded down the side of a sheer cliff.

She picked up her skirts and ran across the fields through the center of the forest of Canda and Figamon trees. When she finally cleared the forest, she entered the field of tall grasses and lazily picked a bouquet of purple Limonas, blue Trimonts, and yellow Sylias. She held the flowers up to her face and inhaled their sweet fragrance. This was such a beautiful place.

Suddenly, the sky blackened and thunder exploded. Lightning arced between the massive thunderheads and scattered like spider webs along the storm's underbelly. Great bolts of lightning streaked from the sky and struck the ground with a sickening splat. The wind gusted, causing the tall grasses to swirl about her.

In the distance, a great ball of fire fell from the heavens and hit the ground. At first, all she heard was a faint rumbling sound when suddenly the sound grew in intensity and volume. The ground shook fiercely as the rumbling slowly faded away.

The green grass at her feet dried up, turned brown and was blown away by the wind as she watched in shocked silence. Next came the screams from the village. She began running back to see what was wrong. Maybe she could help. Maybe.

Snow swirled as it fell from the sky, coating the world in an icy blanket. Things were happening so quickly. The temperature changed drastically and the snow accumulated at her feet. The events around her seemed to be happening in fast-forward.

Then, suddenly, all was silent. She stood in the ruin of what had once been a beautiful paradise. Ice and snow covered everything. The forest of beautiful trees was nothing more than skeletons standing sentinel in the distance. The wildflowers she'd just picked hung lifeless from her hand, the waterfall had frozen.

A small sound reached her ears and she moved toward it. Inside one of the huts, she found a woman huddled in the corner, saying a prayer.

"Merciful Goddess Geno, why have you forgotten your people? What have we done to incur your wrath? Since you see ill fit to gift me, your final follower, with the strength to defeat my enemy.

"I shall call upon your sister the Goddess Lisk, Warrior Matron. Let my arm be strong. Help me to show this vile creature the extent of your wrath and the strength of your fury.

"Help me avenge my people and with my dying breath, I give to you my soul," the woman prayed, over and over until her voice was hoarse and clogged by her tears. The woman rocked back and forth continuously like a frightened child.

That was when she felt it. The evil in the air. The presence of a being so malevolent, it caused shivers to run down her spine. Her heart accelerated in her chest and her breath came in a rush. What was it? What did it want?

Slowly, she turned her head to look over her shoulder. There in the doorway, it stood, just as it had earlier. Only this time, it didn't see her, and it wasn't in human form. It looked more like a mutated beast than anything else. Its red gaze focused unwaveringly on the woman as it ambled forward. Its jaws clicked together. Blood-red liquid dripped from its icy teeth. A low growl bubbled forth from its blood-drenched lips.

Meredith wanted to scream, though she didn't dare. As she watched, the beast ripped the woman to shreds, leaving nothing recognizable behind. Then it turned its feral gaze on her.

Maim. Kill. Destroy. The words echoed in her head over and over again. *Kill them all.*

Meredith squeezed her eyes shut tightly to block out the horrible red glare. She clamped her hands over her ears. Tried to block out the horrible chant echoing in her mind, but still the words repeated over and over. *Maim. Kill. Destroy.* The scream she'd been holding back broke free and rang out in the silence of the night.

Steely hands gripped her arms and she fought them with all her strength. She pushed at the chest before her, expecting to feel an icy cold, but instead found warmth. Her eyes popped open. Her breath whooshed out. Dawson stared down at her and she flung herself into his arms.

She leaned into him, sobbing out her fears and relief. A nightmare. It had only been a nightmare, but it had seemed so very real.

"What is it? What's wrong, baby?"

Meredith shook her head. "It was horrible, Dawson. Truly horrible. All those people. That monster." She cried harder, burying her face in his neck.

He pulled her back and tipped her chin up, forcing her to look at him.

"Tell me what happened?"

"The planet was so beautiful. Peace, harmony, fields of green and roaring waterfalls. Then it came. When its ship crashed on the planet, the atmosphere changed. The grass dried up, the snow began to fall, and the rivers and lakes froze." She pulled her knees up to her chest and curled her arms around them. "He picked the inhabitants off one by one, taking the shape of someone they knew to lure them in. A monster of ice...completely of ice. Fitting for something so cold, isn't it?" Her voice was nothing more than a harsh whisper in the darkness.

"I felt as if I was there, Dawson. I saw it attack a woman. He looked right at me, yet through me."

She went into his arms, snuggling close to his chest. The steady rhythm of his pounding heart was oddly comforting and drowned out the crackling of the fire. She felt safe with him, safer than she'd ever felt with Kaz.

Hopefully, her uncle would come for them before much longer…before they shared the fate of the Genotites.

Dawson kissed her forehead and she smiled in response to his caress. It was in that instant that she began to take notice of his hard, warm body pressed against hers.

Reaching up, she wiped the tears from her eyes and kissed him softly on the chin. "Dawson," she murmured.

"Yes," he replied.

"I don't want to think or talk about my nightmare anymore. I'm tired of being scared all the time. I just want to make love to you," she whispered softly.

He held her tight. "With pleasure, we'll talk when you're ready. Anything you want, baby," he murmured before capturing her lips with his own.

His tongue slipped between her lips, scraped against her teeth and tangled with hers. He pushed the hem of her shirt up, sliding his fingers up her sides in the process. His mouth pulled away from hers just long enough to remove the shirt she wore and toss it away before colliding with her mouth once more.

The air on her skin was cool and his hands were rough, yet gentle. His fingers slid over the swells of her breasts and his thumbs brushed against her taut nipples.

Meredith shivered. Her back arched and she shoved her breasts further into his hands. She ached from head to toe with need and a soft moan escaped her lips. Heat pooled in her lower body and liquid fire began to flow, readying her pussy for him.

She ripped his shirt off and traced her index finger down his chest.

"You know what fascinates me about you? The penchant you have for old-fashioned things, like these jeans."

She knelt and unsnapped his jeans, inching the fabric slowly down until she could reach her prize. She teased his erection with one fingernail. His cock jumped and quivered beneath her explorations and she smiled at his reaction.

Meredith drew in a deep breath and gently blew it out over the tip of his penis. She licked and sucked, kissed and teased, sliding her hand to cup the weight of his balls, until a moan of pleasure burst from his throat.

Her lips kissed his inner thigh as she grabbed his ass and smiled. "Need something?" she murmured.

"You...only you," he rasped out.

Dawson groaned as she licked and suckled his cock. Harder and faster, he pumped his hips, seeking fulfillment. When the tension within him finally broke, he let out a tormented sound as he erupted, spilling his essence into her mouth.

Meredith sat up, licked her lips, enjoying the taste of his come in her mouth. She ran a finger along his shadowed jaw and smiled. "You're getting rough."

He chuckled and smiled in return. "That I am. I didn't scratch you earlier, did I?"

"No, it kind of tickled." She laughed, the nightmare forgotten for the time being.

He caressed her cheek and smoothed back her hair. "Thank you, darlin'. We really should try and get some sleep. You need to rest, we have a long day ahead of us."

* * * * *

Dawson stood in the center of the circle to issue orders for the tasks ahead. "Jacobs, Temple and Bowman, I need the three of you to return to the ship for more supplies. Hanson, you and Timmons go to the skeleton forest and search for more wood. And by all means, *stay together*," he ordered.

Meredith tugged at his sleeve. "Shouldn't you warn them about the monster?" she whispered at his ear.

He didn't want to panic them, but she was right. They needed to know what was out there and the risk they took by leaving camp. "Hold on a sec," he ordered, loud enough for all the men to hear.

"The creature lurking out there is unlike anything we've seen before. We've learned from the encounter Meredith had with it that it's afraid of the fire." He paused a moment, thinking as his gaze drifted to the nearby fire. "I want at least one man with each party carrying a torch."

"Torch, sir?" Hanson asked. "But we don't have any."

"Just a moment." Dawson rushed back inside and came out carrying several strips of material. He grabbed up a long log and wrapped it around the end, then soaked it in alcohol from a bottle in his pocket that he'd grabbed out of Meredith's supplies. Holding the material over the fire, he watched as it caught fire and slowly burned.

"Now you do." He handed it off to Hanson and set to work making another as Timmons stepped up to help him. "Take at least one lit and two extras with you. When one begins to die down, light another one."

"Yes, sir," the group replied, before dispersing to fulfill their assigned tasks.

One group of three headed off in the direction of the crash site, the other two turned and headed into the woods.

* * * * *

The ice creature watched, fully alert, waiting and listening with rapt attention. Opportunity presented itself to him once more. They had separated again, two in the hut, two in the woods and three going off to a place much farther away, making it that much easier to attack.

Beings to kill. He hadn't had this much pleasure since the last of the Genotites had perished at his claws. Their blood, heavily laden with fear, had been the sweetest of nectars…his reason for being, existing.

He could hear the voices in his head once more. The driving need that pushed him to carry out his heinous acts. This was what he lived for, breathed for and had traveled across the universe for—*victims*.

More. More victims. The voices called out. They craved blood, torture, death.

The beings left behind would be an easy target, if not for the fire they possessed. He hated fire, loathed it. It hurt, maimed, marred his beautiful icy form. He calculated his options coldly and decided on the ones out in the open. The smaller group would be the easiest, but the larger one would be better. *Three go farther away. Three more isolated. Three better sate appetite. Save others for later.*

His gaze darted back to the two headed for the skeleton forest one last time before making his way toward the ruined spacecraft. Such a tasty feast had awaited him on his previous visit, but this time a fresh meal was waiting. The voices inside were always demanding, demanding more than he could offer them. This time, the demands could be met slowly. The everlasting, never-ending bloodlust would be fed once more.

He moved silently through the snow, became one with the ice flakes, leaving no trail. The lake of ice lay ahead, but that was not a worry. Sliding, slinking and skating were easy and aided him in his travels.

The three beings traveled in silence through his icy world, leaving their footprints to mar the clean, white snow. His snow. Though it didn't matter. Soon, soon they would be his. His meal, his feast. Before long, they *all* would be.

The beings stopped at the remains of the ship, huddled close together to shield themselves from the wind. They searched. They looked everywhere. They moved around the area, tempting and teasing him.

He badly wanted to attack, to maim, though now was not the time. *Separate. Destroy. Bide time. Enjoy the kill.*

His icy tongue moved out to lick his frozen lips. Just the thought of their heated blood sliding down his throat made him thirsty. *Time to play, to lure, to kill his prey.*

His form shifted to that of a female of their kind. In his lifetime, he'd learned many skills and could adapt to any form, even those foreign to him. The body he chose exhibited soft, feminine curves and long, flowing locks of curling hair. Breasts formed, full and heavy, the nipples erect and begging for male attention.

A soft voice carried on the wind. A siren's song meant to lure in any unsuspecting fool who should happen to hear it.

He didn't have to wait long. One was coming, slowly, reluctantly pulling away from the others. It wouldn't be long until he would feast again.

* * * * *

Jacobs blinked in disbelief when he rounded the corner and spotted her. Where had this woman come from? She was beautiful. A vision of an angel, if ever he'd imagined one. Her long, crystal-clear hair hung down below her waist. High, firm breasts thrust forward invitingly, and the forest of curls at her pussy begged him to come and claim what could be his.

Captain Lang had ordered them to stay together, but even the captain couldn't have resisted such a sweet temptation. He dropped his torch and rushed forward, fumbling with his clothes as he went. He felt like a schoolboy with his first woman, and his eagerness embarrassed him. But he didn't truly care. Claiming her was all that mattered at the moment.

She stood there, still and quiet, arms open wide, welcoming him into their embrace. He fell blindly into those waiting arms, his cock already hard and primed, his heart thundering in his chest.

His gaze moved up to hers and it was then he realized that something was wrong. The feral red glow in her eyes sent shivers down his spine, his heart stuttered as terror took hold.

Her smile transformed from angelic to demonic in the blink of an eye. Her head morphed from soft, feminine features to long, gaping jaws filled with razor-sharp fangs. It hissed and snapped its teeth together, raising its talons high into the air. Ice pellets dropped from the corners of its elongated mouth as its saliva dripped and froze in midair.

The monster lowered its head, and its fangs pierced the throbbing veins in his victim's neck. Its claws dug into the man's arms and held him close to its icy form.

Jacobs tried to scream, but no sound came. His voice was paralyzed in his throat. His body shook in fear. His life flashed before his eyes as he felt the flesh of his neck being ripped out. Then all went black for him.

The creature paid no mind to the limp body in its arms other than the pleasure it gave him to rip the flesh apart. His teeth shredded the soft tissues of the neck and his long, raspy tongue lapped up the sweet, metallic-tasting blood, taking bits of flesh with it.

His long claws ripped at the body, mangled it beyond recognition. Then he feasted on the remains.

The beast dropped what little he had not consumed and moved to a new spot. His next victim worked nearby, oblivious to the danger he was in. Silently, he moved into position as his body shifted once more, repairing the damage caused by the feeding. He drew from the snow to replenish what had been lost to the heat of the attack.

Again the creature sent out his siren's call, lured his victim in. His victim ambled mindlessly toward the beautiful ice maiden the creature projected himself as. The man dropped the fire he'd thought to use as a weapon and continued to move forward. His claws ripped into the flesh of the man's arm and dragged him closer. His prey's eyes were huge in terror, reflecting the red of his own eyes in their depths.

A sound brought the creature's head snapping up. His lips curled back and a growl rumbled forth. In the distance, the third man stood staring at the creature and his meal.

Temple's eyes grew wide with terror as he watched the creature sink its fangs into Bowman's throat. The scene before him frightened him so badly he dropped the torch he held in his hand. The creature before him was unlike anything he'd ever seen. He hesitated before turning tail to run. The terrified man ran as fast as the snow would allow back to camp without daring to look behind.

He fell into the doorway of the hut the captain and Dr. Carson shared, panting for breath. The thundering of his heart shook his body, his face was ashen and he could barely speak.

Dawson helped him to sit up and lean back against one of the cool, stone walls. "What happened? Where are the others?" he asked.

Temple's head shook. "It got them, sir. Ripped them apart. I...I couldn't do anything to stop it," he gasped.

"What? What got them?"

"An ice female," he rasped out, squeezing his eyes shut. "So much blood! So much blood!" Temple's body began to rock back and forth, much the same as Meredith's had the previous day. "Teeth, so many teeth, and those claws! Dead. All dead."

"Temple, it wasn't your fault. No one blames you," he said as he gripped the man's arm. "Did you see Hanson or Timmons on your way back in? They're still out collecting wood."

Temple's head shook as he continued to rock. "No, sir, I saw no one."

"Just relax, Temple. I'll go see if I can find them," Dawson said as he stood.

He went to walk out the door, after he had donned his outerwear, when a hand grasped his arm. Dawson spun around to face Meredith and her blazing green eyes.

"Don't you dare go out there alone. There were three of them and only one came back. I can't bear to lose you. Not now," she told him in a frantic voice. "Not ever."

He pulled her into his arms and kissed her lips. "I'll be okay, darlin'. You just wait here for me."

Meredith's gaze darted to where Temple sat. "His mind is shattered."

Dawson nodded. "I know, but there's not really anything we can do for him. Do you have any suggestions?"

She shook her head. "I hate to think of leaving anyone out here defenseless."

"But is he a danger to the crew?"

She nodded, refusing to look at the other man.

"Temple!" Dawson called, turning his attention to the man. "Do you have any type of restraints on you?"

The other man pulled out a pair of cuffs and held them out in his hand. Before Dawson could order him to turn around so he could place the cuffs on him, Temple slumped over. He furrowed his brow then noticed Meredith standing there beside the now unconscious man.

"What did you do?"

"Tranquilizer. I thought it'd be easier to restain him if he was out cold," she explained.

She was something else. He rolled Temple over and secured the electro-cuffs to his wrists.

Dawson took Meredith by the arms. "You stay right here. I'm going to see if I can find Hanson and Timmons."

"Oh no, you're not. Not with that thing out there. It's clearly not afraid of the fire anymore," she pointed out.

"We don't know what happened. Maybe it frightened them so badly they didn't try to defend themselves."

Meredith scoffed at that. "Even *I* managed to defend myself against it and I was terrified."

Dawson had to find his men and then figure out a plan to kill or elude this beast they'd encountered. They would *not* die on this godforsaken planet. They wouldn't!

He lifted her chin and kissed her gently. "That's because you're special."

"I don't think the creature knows the difference."

Dawson stepped out the door and Meredith chased after him. She grabbed his arm. "I won't let you go out there on your own."

"I'll be fine," he said, turning back toward the forest when he noticed two figures in the distance. "Especially since it seems I don't have a reason to go anywhere. Will you be okay here while I go out to meet them? We'll be within sight the entire time."

Meredith let go of his arms and stepped back. "You just be careful."

He flashed her a grin and headed out to meet up with Timmons and Hanson as she went back inside.

"Sir, what are you doing out here alone?" Timmons asked.

"We've had trouble while the two of you were gone," he replied.

"What happened, sir?" Hanson asked.

"We've lost Jacobs and Bowman, and Temple isn't himself. Let's get back to camp and try to come up with a plan. We have to hold that thing off long enough for the rescue team to get here."

"Isn't himself, sir?" Hanson looked from the captain to Timmons, who shrugged.

"He saw the...creature...thing. I think it was more than his mind could handle," Dawson explain. "I've restrained him, but I still want you to keep a close eye on him. And having said that, let's get back. Meredith's already been alone with him longer than I care for."

The captain turned back toward camp, with Timmons and Hanson falling into step behind him, still carrying the wood. Once there, they all entered the small building and the men placed their burden in a pile along the wall, before dousing their lit torch.

"Well, sir, this should last for a while longer at least," Hanson remarked.

"We can't keep going out for wood. That monster killed two of us today, and we can't go to the woods, because there's no shelter," Dawson remarked.

"Then what do we do, sir?" Timmons asked.

"We must move to the desert region of the planet," Meredith said. "It only makes sense that if it's made of ice, that warmth will keep it at bay." She rubbed her arms and paced beside the fire.

"Apparently carrying torches and even laser pistols is useless, since it still managed to get Jacobs and Bowman. If we go to the desert region, it shouldn't be able to get to us." Though "shouldn't" and "couldn't" were two totally different things.

"They called it a *Kalerian*. It picked off the Genotites one by one until they were extinct. Now, the creature is after us," Meredith whispered in a faraway-sounding voice.

"How do you know this?" Dawson demanded. "How could you possibly know what these people were called? The name of that thing that's out there?"

"I dreamt it. I guess the scratch allowed some connection to the creature, its memories and feelings into my bloodstream, the ability to sense it. It's the only explanation I can think of." Her head shook and her eyes glittered in the flickering light of the fire. "It was almost as if I was there, experiencing what it did. I could hear its thoughts. It fed off the people here and then turned to the planet. That's why this place is dead. It killed it. How...how could anything be that completely evil?"

"I don't know, Meredith," Dawson breathed, pulling her into his arms. He held her tightly against him, stroked her hair. "I don't know."

"Are you sure traveling that far is such a wise idea?" Temple asked, having come to shortly after Hanson and Timmons had arrived, but he didn't question his restraints. He seemed to have shaken off his terror.

"It's afraid of the fire. The desert is hot. Since it's made of ice, it makes sense to go there where it can't follow," Meredith pointed out.

"She has a point, Temple," Dawson remarked.

"But how do we keep that thing off us while we travel? It can move in the snow and ice like we can on a paved road back home. It didn't seem all that afraid of the fire when it was ripping Bowman apart, and I seriously doubt that a pistol would have slowed it down. Besides, there are only five of us left," Temple shot back. His fear-driven words sounding more harshly disrespectful than they normally would have been. "What of the rescue ship? Do we even know if they're sending one?"

"They'll come," Meredith replied through gritted teeth.

"What makes you so sure of that?" he asked.

"Because Kaz won't leave us here. So long as there's hope that I survived, he'll come," she remarked.

There she goes again. Who in hell is this Kaz person she keeps referring to? Dawson thought. What was this guy to her? She already owned his heart, his body. She claimed to care for him, but did she? Or did she really belong to this Kaz fellow and had just fallen into his arms because of the dire situation they found themselves in?

"Grab what you can. There should be plenty of daylight left to travel in. We'll carry torches too, just in case." Dawson said.

"Yes, sir!" Timmons and Hanson said in unison.

Temple looked at the small group as if they'd lost their minds. "Yes, sir, though I can't carry anything while cuffed," he remarked. They knew that what he'd seen had affected him greatly, but to exactly what extent they didn't know.

"Then you just won't carry anything, because the cuffs are staying on," Dawson told him.

Dawson moved over to Meredith who had slipped on her coat while he had been giving orders. He pulled up her collar, moved her hood into place, fastened it and helped her to button up her coat. "It's extremely cold out there. Don't want you getting sick on us, now do we?"

"Thank you," she murmured.

He leaned forward and gently kissed her lips.

"Oh, cut the lovey-dovey stuff out, will you?" Temple grumbled.

Dawson spun on the man so quickly that no one saw him move. He pointed at the other man while visibly vibrating with anger. "I'd advise you to watch the attitude, mister," he growled. He wanted to say more, but the looks on Meredith, Hanson and Timmons's faces stopped him cold.

"We could always leave him," Hanson suggested.

Temple glared at Hanson.

"No, we couldn't. No one is left behind," Dawson replied in a calmer tone. "Gather up your gear and let's get the hell out of here."

"Sir, I apologize for being out of line. I'm still shaken from the earlier incident," he replied.

"Everyone ready?" Dawson asked. "There looks to be a storm brewing on the horizon, I want to at least make it back to the *Drigon* before it hits." They all nodded and mumbled "yes". "Then let's go," he ordered, leading the way out the door and into the cold.

He kept Meredith by his side the entire time. They led the way through the snow, back toward the fallen ship, glancing over their shoulders occasionally to make sure the others still followed. Hanson and Timmons were just behind them, and Temple brought up the rear, his eyes constantly scanning the horizon.

* * * * *

In the distance, just out of sight, the creature followed in their wake. Its nostrils flared, inhaling their mingled scents. He'd marked the female. Tainted her with his scratch. He could track her anywhere...anywhere at all.

No one had ever escaped his clutches. No one—yet she had somehow managed to get away. He couldn't let that happen, couldn't allow her to be free. If she left the planet, she'd tell his previous captors where he was. No more prison ships, no more entrapment. He was free, and that was the way he would stay.

He knew where they were going. Why they were going. But it was useless. They could not hide. He was able to adapt, to change and to fit all environments. In his other form their heat and fire would not hurt. But his prey did not know that. Not even with the female's visions. He continued to follow them, biding his time. The longer he waited, the greater their fear and the better the feast.

Chapter Nine

ॐ

The storm moved in fast and furious. The snow swirled so hard they could barely see. Dawson paused to look back at his men. The remains of the *Drigon* lay just ahead. Though it wouldn't be very warm, the ship's hull would at least provide some shelter from the gusting winds.

He raised his hand up over his head and waved to draw the men's attention, then pointed toward the ship. Each man nodded in understanding, and Dawson turned to lead the way through the blinding snow.

Dawson entered the bridge first. He had to be sure nothing waited for them inside. After he'd made sure it was clear, he pulled Meredith in from the cold.

"Go sit down up front while we work on getting the doors closed. It'll still be cold, but at least the wind can't reach us and, hopefully, we'll lock whatever that thing is outside," he told her.

"Okay." Slowly, she made her way through the dimly lit interior of the bridge. The controls seemed to be pretty much in one piece, though there were several wires hanging out. If she remembered correctly, the cabin had its own life-support system. Maybe…

* * * * *

Dawson, Hanson and Timmons worked on sealing the doors as Temple stood back and watched. With Temple's hands still cuffed, he wasn't much help to them.

The doors finally slammed shut with a loud metallic clang, and the men fell against it exhausted. Sweat beaded on Dawson's forehead and he noticed the temperature was warmer than it had been. Surely, he hadn't worked himself up that much with the doors?

Meredith appeared a short while later grinning, without her coat. "Looks like Kaz's technology classes have paid off."

Dawson's eyebrow rose. "How'd you…?" he began.

"The bridge has its own life-support system for such an occurrence, as you know. Now, as Timmons reported shortly after the crash, the primary power core is cracked. They had shut it down. I just turned it back on and flipped the proper switches," she answered before he was finished speaking.

"Well, I'll be damned. A medic and a mechanic. Maybe allowing you onboard wasn't such a bad idea after all." Dawson grinned. "I had my doubts."

"It won't last long, but we should be able to make it through the night with at least some warmth." She worried her bottom lip with her teeth. "It's a good thing we didn't stay, though, and we have to leave as soon as possible."

"Why?" Dawson asked.

"There's a slight radiation leak. Short-term exposure shouldn't leave any lasting damage, but if we stay too long—"

He nodded. "We'll leave as soon as the storm is over, and it's light. I don't want to be out there in the dark."

Temple mumbled something incoherently and Dawson glared at him. The man was really getting to be a pain in the ass. Scared out of his wits or not, being rude to Meredith wasn't acceptable.

Temple turned away from the captain's stare and huddled in a corner, keeping to himself.

Meredith glanced between the two men, cautiously, before speaking again. "I tried to raise the deflector plates off the front window, but the controls are jammed and won't budge. It will probably be warmer with them closed, but I thought it would be better to watch what the storm's doing and if we're being followed."

"That's all right. If we get too curious, we can just toss Temple out for a progress report," Dawson remarked as he glared at the man in the corner. To hell with Alliance protocol. This was his ship, he wasn't a true leader and he was fed up with this shit.

Meredith moved to where Dawson stood and placed her hand on his arm. "He's not right since earlier, Dawson. You can't hold him accountable for his actions," she whispered.

He kissed her forehead. "Perhaps."

"You'd better get out of this coat before you burn up," she remarked, tugging at the buttons.

He gave her a lopsided grin and leaned closer. "Darlin', I'm already burning up, and you're more than welcome to strip me anytime, anywhere you like," he whispered at her ear.

Meredith felt the heat creep into her cheeks. "I-I...need to go check on something. You should check the emergency beacon and make sure it's still working."

"You mean you can't do it?" he asked with a raised eyebrow.

"I was absent that day," she replied with a sly smile.

Timmons and Hanson chuckled at the byplay but didn't say a word. Each thought it was good that the captain had finally found some happiness, even if it might be his last.

Dawson turned his gaze to his chuckling men and glared.

"Don't mind us, sir," Timmons replied. "We're just going to sit here and enjoy the heat."

"Yeah. The heat," Hanson replied. He had his head leaned back against the door and his eyes closed. "I was beginning to forget what heat felt like."

"I'll be back shortly," Dawson warned.

Timmons winked at him. "Oh, don't rush on our account. Take all the time you need."

Stalking farther into the bridge, he moved to where the beacon sat on top of the control panel. He checked all the connections and made sure it still functioned properly. Meredith had disappeared while he worked, only to reappear in the door to his cabin.

"What are you doing in there?" he asked.

"Rummaging through your stuff. What else?" she asked, a smile curving her delicate lips up at the corners. Her eyes sparkled with mischief as she gazed at him.

"Find anything of interest?" Anyone else would have had their ears reddened from the scathing lecture he'd have given, but he found the idea of her going through his property somewhat appealing. Hell, it turned him on.

"I think so," she said as she held up a small square box. "Something to keep the boys occupied."

She sashayed past him and walked back to where the others still sat against the wall. "Here, Hanson, I brought you something," she said.

He popped his eyes open, and she tossed the box at him. He caught it in his hands and looked at it a second before a wide grin spread across his face.

"Cards! Why thank you, ma'am."

Timmons quickly opened his eyes at the excitement in Hanson's voice. "Where did you get cards, Doc?" he asked.

"I pillaged the captain's quarters," she laughed.

"And still breathing to tell the tale. Imagine that," Hanson remarked, shaking his head. "Ow!" he cried out when Timmons elbowed him in the ribs. "I didn't mean anything by it." He rubbed his side and glared at Timmons.

Meredith smirked. "I'm sure you didn't. No worries. Need anything else?"

"A big, thick, juicy steak would be nice," Hanson remarked.

"And a big baked tater with the works," Timmons piped in.

"Oh, yes, can't forget that," Hanson agreed. "And a giant glass of frothy beer. Yep, think I would be in heaven if I had those."

"Wouldn't we all?" Meredith laughed.

"Guess we'll have to be satisfied with a tin of beans and the mystery meat package," Hanson grumbled.

"I'm getting away from you two. I'll be dreaming of steak every time I close my eyes from here on out, thanks to you," Meredith said as she walked away.

"You're welcome," they called out in unison.

Meredith was still laughing when she rejoined Dawson up front.

"What was that all about?" he asked, eyeing her as she walked across the room.

"Steak, baked potato and beer," she replied with as straight a face as possible.

Dawson's stomach growled at the words and he slapped a big hand against it. "Don't talk like that. I'm already sick of whatever is in those rations."

She doubled over laughing.

"What's so funny?" he demanded.

"The men call it mystery meat," she pointed out. Meredith wiped the tears from her eyes with the back of her hand.

"Laugh it up, woman. I'm starving," he grumbled.

"So am I," she replied in a husky voice. She smiled seductively at him.

She moved past where he stood and headed into his quarters, pausing in the doorway. Glancing over her shoulder, she winked, blew him a kiss and disappeared into the darkness.

Dawson stood there staring after her for several long seconds before following her. A dim red glow filtered over the room from the emergency lights that had come on when she'd rigged the life support. Meredith stood by the bed, digging in his bedside table drawer.

"What are you doing?" he asked, hands on hips.

She glanced over her shoulder at him and held up his holo-shades. "Just looking." Tossing the shades over her shoulder, she returned to the drawer and its contents.

"Anything in particular you're searching for?"

She peered up at him through her lashes and a smile graced her lips. She held up something in the dim light.

Dawson felt his heart stop and heat creeping into his cheeks. He couldn't believe she'd found that. Would she think him odd for having a tube of lube in his drawer?

"Been having a little fun, have we?" she murmured, turning to face him. She held the tube in her hands, running her fingers along its edges. Her smile grew wider, and she wiggled her eyebrows at him.

"Why do I feel you're looking for a certain answer from me?"

Meredith laughed. "I'm not asking for confessions, Dawson. I just wanted to see your reaction." She wiggled the tube in her hand. "So, ah—wanna play?"

He raised an eyebrow at her. "Play? How?"

She laughed at the caution in his voice, tossed him the tube and started stripping quickly. A seductive smile curved her lips as she looked up at him. "Are you just going to stand there, or are you going to join me?"

He looked behind him toward where the men were. "Won't they be able to hear?"

Meredith shrugged. "So? What if I promise to be quiet?" She pooched her lip out in a pout.

She didn't know where this sudden burst of bravery came from, but it felt good. If they were to die on this planet, at least she'd die knowing Dawson's touch. She wanted him in every way a woman could love her man.

He watched her as she lay back on the bed and spread her legs for him. Her hand slithered down her body and parted the folds of her pussy, inviting him in.

His cock grew harder with each passing caress as he watched her fingers move over her clit and slip into her heat. Her head fell back and she moaned as she rubbed her mound.

With quick, jerky movements, he shed his clothes and moved to stand over her. His eyes moved over her from head to toe, lingering on the motions of her fingers at her pussy. "That's it, baby, fuck yourself."

"I want you," she said in a husky voice.

"Want me how?"

"Any way you want." She pushed her fingers inside her pussy once more. A fine tremor caused her legs to shake as she hit just *that* spot.

He slid his hands slowly up her legs and over her stomach, stroked her breasts, bringing her nipples to peaks. He leaned over and captured her mouth with his, kissing her hungrily, as if he was starving.

Hot, wet kisses trailed along her cheek, down her neck, then his teeth bit gently at her earlobe. He moved his hands over hers, pressing them, encouraging her movements.

Dawson gave her a devilish grin before coaxing her to roll over onto her stomach. He pulled her hips, urging her to climb up onto her knees. Then he knelt down and leaned forward, inhaling her feminine fragrance, tasting her juices.

He moaned and licked the lips of her pussy, sending tiny thrills of pleasure vibrating through her. Meredith sensually circled her hips then moved back and forth enticing him to do more. She leaned forward, withdrawing from him then pushed back to get closer.

His hand moved up, his fingers pinched gently the hard nub of her clit, delved into her liquid fire. His tongue pushed into her, lapping at her juices as she continued to rock against him. Fingers continued to circle her clit while his other hand grabbed her hip, speeding her grinding actions.

Meredith moved her hand to twist at one nipple, and then pinched at the other. She sucked her bottom lip into her mouth and worried at it with her teeth as the pressure built within her body. The hairs on his face pricked her sensitive flesh, heightened the sensations she felt. The things he did to her felt exciting, but she found herself needing, craving, more.

"Dawson," she cried out.

His lips pressed against her as he sucked, pulling her skin closer to him. He kissed the folds of her pussy, broke the suction and leaned back.

"What? What do you want, Meredith? What do you need?"

"More."

"What more?" he asked, his voice nearly as husky as her own.

"Everything," she moaned. "Everything you have to give."

He licked her upper thigh and slapped one cheek of her ass as he rose to his feet. Retrieving the tube of lubrication from the bed, he squirted a glob on his finger and traced circles around the puckered opening of her anus. Slowly, he inserted one finger into the opening, stretching her with his invasion.

Meredith moaned and the upper half of her body lowered to the bed, raising her ass higher toward him. She pushed against his finger, taking more in, until he had no more to offer. Slowly, her body took up a rocking motion, pushing against his finger.

Dawson watched her, measured her reaction before slowly inserting another finger to join the first. He pushed against her each time she pushed back, in an attempt to help her find what she sought.

"It's not enough, is it, Meredith?" he asked, kissing her on the small of her back.

"No." Her voice sounded strangled, almost as if the sound had been ripped from her throat.

He withdrew his hand, and she groaned in displeasure. Dawson watched her push back, seeking him out.

Squeezing another glob from the tube, he smeared the gel over his erection. His hands were slick from the gel as he slid them over her hips, pulling her back within his reach.

She could feel the hard length of his cock pressed against the opening of her ass. The stretching sensation overwhelmed her when she moved back to meet his hips. She ground her hips in a circular pattern, enticing him to do more than rub against her with his penis.

Dawson slid the tip of his cock over her backside, gripping her hip with his other hand. Allowing just the tip to enter her pussy, he stopped and flexed his fingers at her hips.

"Is this what you want? Indulge me, tell me where?"

She shook her head. "No, it's not what I want."

"Then what is it? Tell me."

Meredith wasn't sure she could tell him, but she could certainly show him. She withdrew from him, pulling free of his cock. Reaching beneath her, she caressed the underside of his erection with her fingertips, her nails. Arching her back, she grasped his cock and guided it to where she wanted him.

He slid his finger in her pussy, getting it drenched in her juices, then pressed it against the opening of her anus. "Here, sweetheart?" He slowly slid his finger inside and she pushed back against him at the same time. "Mm," he murmured, withdrawing from her once more.

Meredith moaned and pushed back harder. "Dawson, please?"

He grabbed her hips, rubbing her flesh against his cock. "Yes?"

"Do it!" She ground out between clenched teeth.

"Do what?" he asked, moving her forward and positioning the tip of his penis against her opening. "This?"

He pushed, slowly entering her, stretching her.

He thrust gently, gritting his teeth as her body absorbed his, until his balls touched her ass. His fingers gripped and relaxed on her hips as he paused, trying to control himself long enough to allow her time to adjust to his penetration.

When Meredith moved, pulling free of him, the action surprised him. His breath sucked in as she pulled free of all but the tip of his cock then pushed back, taking him in once more. With each movement she made, the speed of her actions increased. His hips slammed against her ass, his cock driving into her as they both strove for fulfillment. Over and over again they continued the push and pull of their lovemaking, increasing the tension with each stroke, each connection of flesh to flesh.

Dawson tightened his grip, holding her up, looking at his dick as it penetrated her ass. He continued to pump into her. Harder and harder he plunged, bringing cries of pleasure and surprise from her.

He grunted and groaned with each slam of his body until his grip tightened and his body strained. When he felt the orgasm convulse through her, he pulled back on her hips, thrust into her one last time as his seed spilled into her willing warmth and his breath rushed out of his lungs.

Sweat ran down his face, stung his eyes and matted his hair to his forehead. He leaned against her, propping his forehead in the center of her back as he gasped for breath.

Meredith wiggled beneath him, enjoying the feel of him still joined to her and the aftermath of the explosive orgasm that had overtaken her. His breath at her back tickled and cooled her sweat-covered skin.

Slowly, he lifted himself up and withdrew, leaving her feeling bereft. With what little strength she still had, Meredith rolled onto her back and stared up at him through sated eyes.

Her arms rose, beckoned him down to her.

Dawson fell into her arms, curling against her on his bed. His lips kissed her cheek, her ear. "I didn't hurt you, did I?"

She could hear the concern in his voice and she smiled as her head shook. "No. Never," she whispered. "Promise me forever, Dawson." Her eyes fluttered closed as he pulled her tighter against him, her breathing becoming more even as she drifted into sleep.

"Forever, Meredith," he whispered against her hair. "Forever."

Chapter Ten

ॐ

"It's morning and the storm has let up. We'd better get moving soon," Dawson whispered at her ear, before sucking the tip into his mouth.

"How do you know the storm's let up?"

"Instinct."

She tried to wiggle away from him, but his arm wrapped around her waist and pressed his morning erection tightly up against her. "Oh, no, you don't. You're not running from me," he growled at her ear.

Meredith rolled over to face him and placed a hand on his chest. "Dawson, like you said, we need to get moving. I don't want us exposed to the radiation from the cracked core any longer than necessary."

He sighed. "Okay, you win," he reluctantly replied. "Get dressed, honey. The sooner we get started the better. I want to make the desert by nightfall."

She slid from the bed and slipped into her pants, then pulled one of his thick, long-sleeved shirts from one of his drawers. "Do you think we can make it that far?"

"If the weather holds out and you can keep up, we should be able to." He sounded as though he was teasing and he had a sly grin on his face. But Meredith knew there was truth behind his words. She was shorter than the others, considerably so, and, in effect, she would indeed slow them down.

She threw an extra shirt at him, which he deftly caught. "I can keep up with any one of you," she shot back, trying to hide her doubts from him.

He stood and tugged up his jeans, fastening the snap as he walked up behind her. Two large bare arms wrapped around her middle and pressed her back against his naked chest.

"I didn't mean anything by it," he whispered at her ear.

She shrugged out of his hold and turned to look up at him. She lowered her eyes to his chest. "I know. It's just… It makes me want to be something that I'm not. That's why I'm here. I wanted to be someone else. You get tired of having your life planned out for you and being told what to do all the time. I wanted to get away, to experience new things, to have a life of my own," she explained.

"Is that why you insisted on going with us after the first attack? To prove a point?" he asked.

She glared up at him. "Did I prove a point? Or did I reinforce your bad opinion of me? I'm a single woman aboard a ship of nearly forty men. I have more to prove than the others do."

Dawson sighed. "Meredith, I wish I could tell you what I really feel, what I really think, but this isn't the time or the place… I'll tell you one thing, though."

"And what is that?"

He smiled weakly and shook his head. "You don't have anything to prove. If you really want to know my opinion, I thought you handled yourself remarkably well. I know seasoned officers who'd have buckled down when seeing so much blood, and even more if they had to examine a mangled body, but not you. You just kept on going, doing your job as you've been trained to do."

"You don't know how badly I wanted to throw up." She laughed without humor. "I swallowed down my fear, fought the knot in my stomach and did what I had to do."

"Mere, that was enough to gag even the hardest of career officers. You weren't the only one sickened by it. That thing..." he began.

"That thing is pure evil. I'm really beginning to wonder if we are going to make it off this planet alive. But if we...if it does get us, I pray that it gets me first. I couldn't stand to be alone on this planet without you."

"Oh, God," he ground out, closing the small distance she'd placed between them. He pulled her roughly into his arms and captured her lips with his. "Baby, we're going to make it. Do you hear me? I won't let anything happen to either of us. Promise."

"You had better not." Her fisted hand beat at his chest as she cried out her fear and frustration.

He held her until her tears stopped, and then he pushed her back to look at her. The back of his finger moved over her cheek, wiping away the last traces of her tears.

"Come on, darlin'. Let's dry those tears and get moving. You finish straightening yourself up and I'm going to try communications before we go," he told her.

Meredith nodded her head. "Okay. I'll be done in a few minutes."

Dawson exited the room and headed over to the comms unit, which had its own small power supply. He pushed a button on the dimly lit screen. It flickered a few times before it faded completely out. "Damn it," he muttered.

He tried thumping the front of it, but nothing happened. *Oh, what the heck.* He popped it hard on its top with his fist. It flickered once more but remained on.

"This is the IPA *Drigon*. Anyone out there? Repeat, this is the IPA *Drigon*. We're stranded on the planet Ferraven. Need immediate assistance," he said.

He held his breath, waiting for a response, but static was his only reply.

"No luck?" she asked.

"No, I'm afraid not. You ready to go?"

She nodded. "Ready as I will ever be."

Dawson ran a hand lovingly over the hull. A brief flash of pain and regret washed over his face at the thought of leaving the *Drigon* behind, but it couldn't be helped. He had to get Meredith someplace safe. Someplace where that *thing* couldn't get to her.

He got up from his broken chair and walked to where she stood. His hand captured hers and he led her to where the others waited, dressed for travel.

"Let's get started. I'd like to make it to the desert before nightfall," he said to his men.

Each nodded, except Temple. He stared blankly at the group and allowed everyone to exit the ship before falling into step behind them.

They had just left the ship when the radio crackled to life.

"IPA *Drigon*...McAllister...coming...position?" a voice called out over the comms unit. But no one was there to respond to the message.

* * * * *

The sun slowly traveled across the sky as they trudged through the snow. They pushed onward without stopping until their surroundings began to slowly change. In the distance, the peaks rose up in shades of browns and grays instead of white. The desert was just ahead. They'd made it!

"Do you think it's safe to undo his hands?" Dawson asked Meredith as they neared the sandy patch up ahead.

"He seems to be more in control of himself today. Go ahead," she replied.

"Temple!" Dawson called, watching as the man drew nearer. "Turn around so I can undo your hands."

Temple obliged him. Once the cuffs were removed, Temple rubbed each wrist in turn. "Thank you, sir," he softly murmured.

"Let's keep moving," Dawson said. "We've almost reached safety."

The snow finally dispersed and muddy patches of sand could be seen in stark contrast to the white snow. The desert loomed up before them, a welcome sight for weary eyes.

Temple rushed forward. "Heat. We're safe!" he yelled as loudly as he could. He dropped his pack and spun in circles in the sand.

Suddenly, the ground began to shake and a low rumble could be heard. Something moved beneath the ground, and it headed straight for them. A line of sand pushed upward and raced toward the jubilant and blissfully unaware Temple.

Meredith screamed. They all yelled at once. Their voices were a cacophony of sound warning Temple to move, to get out of the way.

The next few moments went by in slow motion. Temple turned to face his fellow crewmembers. They could see his eyes grow wide in terror at the sight of the creature rapidly heading toward him. He began to run, but he wasn't fast enough. Temple hadn't taken three steps when the ground beneath his feet exploded in a spray of sand and dirt.

Debris flew nearly twenty feet up into the air and spewed out in every direction. The ground shook as the beast roared.

Temple screamed. Then all fell silent.

The ground vibrated violently. Blood-tinged sand spewed up into the air as a horrifying roar echoed across the land.

When the dust settled, the creature stood before them, red eyes glowing and teeth bared. It looked different, now made of sand instead of ice, but they knew it to be the same creature.

Long jaws extended forward and held huge fangs. Red, laser-like eyes moved over the small group as a feral growl burst out into the air. Claw-tipped hands were held up in front of the beast, its feet appeared to be a part of the sand on which it stood.

"Run," Dawson shouted, snapping them out of the shock-induced trance they'd been in.

Dawson grabbed Meredith's arm. He pulled her with him to the creature's right, keeping himself between her and it while Timmons and Hanson went the other way.

The beast counteracted by sweeping its long, sandy tail across their path, knocking the four off their feet.

"Move!" Dawson yelled, thrusting Meredith back to her feet.

He rolled and jumped to his feet, shoving Meredith along as he went. They had to get away.

Overhead, a storm began to brew. Thick black clouds suddenly appeared on the horizon. Lightning arced from cloud to cloud and scattered across the storm's underbelly like spider webs. Thunder boomed and rumbled as the storm grew in strength, intensity.

The beast roared again, as if in competition with the thunder. A large clawed hand raked at Timmons and Hanson, ripping at their arms and anything else it could reach.

Meredith stopped and Dawson ran into her back, surprised by her sudden halt. Her eyes darted over the land. Something within her told her that she was close. Lightning flashed and she found what she sought.

A short distance away, almost completely concealed by the sand, a metal object lay on the ground. She knew it was the creature's crashed ship. *You marked me, bastard, but I know your secrets.*

She rushed forward and grabbed a metal rod that had broken away from the ship. "Dawson," she called out. He looked over at her and she tossed him the rod. "Aim for the heart."

The *heart*? How in hell was he to know where the heart was? He turned to face the beast, moving closer than he really cared to.

Red eyes turned in his direction, and he could have sworn it smirked at him. His heart thundered in his chest and he found it hard to breathe. He drew back his arm, aimed for what he hoped to be the heart and threw the rod with all his strength.

The metal sliced through the creature's chest, dead center. Its hands moved to the rod to pull it free, but the lightning chose that moment to strike the metal. The red eyes went brighter and then faded until all light was gone from them.

They watched as the creature fell over backwards in seemingly slow motion. The ground shook with the impact and another lightning bolt struck the rod.

Dawson turned to Meredith. "How'd you know to do that?" he asked.

"Sand turns to glass when it gets hot enough," she grinned. She sighed with relief and leaned into him. "Is it really over?"

He looked down at the top of her head then over to the creature. "Yeah, I think it is."

"Hello, down there. Need a lift?" a voice called out.

Dawson and Meredith raised their heads to see a shuttlecraft above them. Meredith smiled at the sight of Kaz hanging out the door.

"Oh, yes," she yelled back, sounding a bit exasperated.

When the ship landed, a small group of men disembarked and moved out to help the wounded Timmons and Hanson into the vessel.

"Kaz!" Meredith yelled, and flew into the arms of the man walking toward her.

Dawson's insides churned. *Kaz?* Kaz was none other than K.C. McAllister. Damn it, she was with the general. How could he ever compete with him?

His heart seemed heavier and his spirits fell. All his dreams and hopes of a future with Meredith had just gone up in smoke. What would he do now?

He watched her every move, and a new light began to shine deep within his eyes. No, he wouldn't give up. He'd fight for her because she was definitely worth it. All he had to do was come up with a plan, one that would work.

He followed the others into the ship, glancing over his shoulder to where the creature had fallen one last time. For some reason, he felt like it had died too easily. He shrugged off the thought and stepped into the cargo bay of the ship, listening to the comforting sound of the door clanging closed behind him.

The ride out of the planet's atmosphere went much smoother than their entrance into it had been. As they circled over the remains of the *Drigon*, a great sense of loss washed over Dawson. He would never see his ship again, but they had managed to survive against the odds.

"Sorry about your ship, Lang. It's always sad to see one fall," General McAllister remarked from across the way as he gazed out the window.

"Thank you, sir," Dawson replied. He swallowed hard. Kind words from the general were the last thing he'd expected to hear. He certainly didn't want a reason to like the man.

Intense blue eyes watched Meredith from across the bay. She laughed and chattered away at McAllister. Dawson felt his jealousy rising once more.

Stop watching them, you fool, you're doing nothing but torturing yourself. You don't have a snowball's chance in hell of stealing her away from McAllister. Dawson shook his head trying to free himself of his disturbing thoughts. *I have a chance with her; he's no better than I am. I can and will win her back.*

With his decision made, he proceeded to check on his men. The journey had been long and hard, but they'd pulled through and beaten the monster. A part of him still was uneasy, but he quickly banished the thought. They were on their way home. That was the only thing he cared about. Well, that and Meredith's safety.

"How are they?" he asked.

"They'll be fine, sir, just as soon as we get back to the ship and can get them to the med lab," one of the attendants replied.

"That's good to hear. Hold tight, Timmons, Hanson," he murmured, then returned to his seat. They'd be docking soon.

A short time later, a small jolt and a loud click signified they had arrived onboard their rescue ship. He briefly wondered its name, but it didn't really matter. She wasn't the *Drigon*, no matter how badly he wished her to be.

The cargo bay doors slowly opened, and Dawson stepped out onto the deck. A crewmember ran up and stopped abruptly in front of him to salute.

"Welcome aboard the IPA *Phoenix*, sir. Glad to have you and the others aboard," the man said.

Dawson motioned with his hand for the man to lower his. "That's not necessary, son," he said.

He stepped down off the ramp and allowed the others to be brought off the shuttle into the *Phoenix*. Even he had to admit that she appeared to be a good-looking ship.

"Lang!" a voice called out from behind him.

His gaze turned to face the general. "Sir?"

"What happened down there?" McAllister moved closer, leaving Meredith to wander around the cargo hold on her own. "What happened to those men?"

"Some life form, sir. It had the ability to change its shape and composition from ice to sand. It killed everyone but us."

"How many survived the crash?"

Dawson's head dropped and he sighed. "Only eleven, sir. From the reports I gathered just after the crash, a large number of the crew were in the mess hall when we went down. It was one of the sections to break away."

McAllister nodded and clapped a hand on Dawson's shoulder. "I'm sorry. It's hard enough to lose a ship, but to lose her crew as well..." He allowed his words to die away. No words could ease the ache left in a captain's heart at the loss of his ship and her crew. He turned his gaze to the crewman Dawson had been speaking to. "Take Captain Lang to his quarters. I'm sure he could use some rest, or at least some time alone."

The crewman nodded. "Yes, sir." His gaze then moved to Dawson. "If you'll follow me, sir, I'll show you to your quarters," the man said with a nod of his head.

He didn't really care to be alone with his thoughts, but oddly enough, the thought of private quarters gave him an idea. "Okay, lead the way, and while you're at it, I have a few questions I'd like to ask you," Dawson replied as he fell into step alongside of the young man.

"Of course, sir. Ask away."

"You see, I have this lady friend," Dawson began, pointing to Meredith as she walked down the ramp. "I want to impress her. Do something romantic. Any suggestions?" he asked.

"No, sir. I wouldn't have a clue, but I think I might know someone who can help you," the man replied.

"Lead the way, man. I've got a lady to impress," Dawson said with a smile.

Chapter Eleven

&

"You want me to what?" Dawson nearly yelled at the woman in front of him.

"You want to impress her, don't you? I find that music is often a doorway to the soul. Try it. What is the worst that can happen?" Miss Jansen said.

"She'll laugh her ass off, that's what can happen," he mumbled.

"Then make her a bouquet of flowers in the replicator and hope it is enough, sir." Was it his imagination or had the woman sounded a bit sarcastic and aggravated with him?

He put his hands on his hips and glared at her. "I'm not going to make a fool of myself by dancing around and crooning a song when I can't dance and can't carry a tune."

"If I might be so bold to explain, sir, in many races and cultures, singing and dancing is used to court their intended. But—very well, sir, we'll just have to think of something else." She placed her hands at her waist and moved away.

"What song did you have in mind, Miss Jansen?" he sighed, defeated.

Her gaze swung back around to his and the first smile he'd seen from her graced her lips. "Well, it is a true oldie, but I think it will be just perfect," she said. She moved to the desk and pressed a button on the computer console.

Instantly, music filled the room. "Oh, and here. I took the courtesy of replicating you a microphone."

"Microphone? And I do what with this exactly?"

"You sing into it, dear," she replied, patting him on the arm.

Dawson ignored her insubordinate tone and had to admit, the tune was catchy, though he still had trouble picturing himself singing. He took the microphone and quirked a brow, but said nothing. He then followed Jansen's lead in dance steps and the lyrics for what seemed an eternity before she deemed him ready to perform for his ladylove.

"Are you sure?" he asked, raising an eyebrow at the woman.

"You are as good as you're likely to get, sir. There is nothing more I can do. God help us," she answered. He watched her move to the replicator and press a button. She reached inside and pulled out a bouquet of red roses. "But just in case, it never hurts to have a backup." She smiled and winked at him.

"Thanks," he mumbled, taking the flowers from her hand.

"She's alone in the canteen. We made sure to keep everyone out so that you can have some privacy." She turned to walk away then paused. "Oh, and one more thing, Captain."

"What's that?" he questioned.

"Shave. A clean-shaven face is less abrasive, Captain Lang," she replied.

He reached up a hand and rubbed it across his chin, then chuckled. "I suppose you have a point there." He watched her go before placing the flowers on the table and heading into the bathroom to take care of his whiskers.

* * * * *

Meredith sat alone at a table sipping a cup of steaming black coffee. She wondered where Dawson could be hiding. If she didn't know better, she'd think he was avoiding her.

The lights in the canteen suddenly dimmed and her gaze darted around the room. Soft music filtered in, and a strangely familiar voice started to sing.

She jerked around in her seat and blinked repeatedly. When her eyes adjusted to the dim lights, they grew wide in shock. Her mouth fell open and she seriously considered pinching herself to be sure she wasn't dreaming.

"Baby, I need you in my arms," he crooned, severely off-key. "Right where I know you belong."

Meredith buried her face in her hands and tried desperately not to laugh. Where had he dug up that relic, and how long had it taken him to find it? She moved her fingers to peek between them. Her attempts at restraint were foiled when a bout of laughter escaped her.

He danced over chairs and tabletops, singing away and shaking his hips, clutching a bouquet of roses in one hand and a microphone in the other. "You're the one for me, the only one I see. You're the one I need, baby, say you'll stay with me," he sang out.

She wasn't even sure he was getting the words right, but it didn't really matter. Right or wrong, the words meant the world to her. He did care. He truly did care about her in his own way.

Meredith jumped to her feet and nearly knocked him over when she threw her arms around him. Her lips met his and cut off the next line he was attempting to sing.

"Oh, Dawson," she breathed. "That was wonderful."

He kissed her back, briefly, then pushed her back. "I wasn't finished yet."

She laughed at the look on his face. "Quit while you're ahead — you got your point across."

The lights suddenly came back up and Meredith stood on tiptoe to look over Dawson's shoulder. She waved and smiled weakly.

"Hey, Kaz," she said.

"What's going on here?" McAllister asked from behind Dawson.

Dawson swallowed, and then turned to face his superior officer, handing the flowers to Meredith in the process. "I was just entertaining the lady, sir," he replied.

Meredith giggled and inhaled deeply. The roses smelled so sweet. "A fine job you did too," she said, giving him a wink. She moved out from behind Dawson and walked over to where McAllister stood. Going up on tiptoe, she kissed his cheek. "Hey, Kaz. How's it going?"

Jealousy surged through Dawson once more. He felt his temperature rise and his temper begin to boil. His heart rate went into double-time and he seriously considered punching McAllister right then and there.

Meredith could feel a change in the air. Something was wrong, but she didn't know what. She turned and gazed at Dawson.

"What's wrong with you?" she asked. Her face showed her concern.

Dawson's temper snapped. "What's this guy to you?" he asked, pointing at the general.

Meredith pointed over her shoulder with her thumb. "You mean Kaz? He's my uncle, Dawson. What did you think?"

"Uncle?" he repeated. "He's your uncle?"

McAllister reached out and rubbed Meredith's shoulder. "Darling, why don't you go back to your room, so that Captain Lang and I can have a talk."

She turned to look at him over her shoulder. "I'm not so—" she began.

"It'll be okay, darling. I won't hurt him," Kaz said with a wink and a wicked smile.

"You'd better not," she warned, pointing a finger at him. Her gaze moved back to Dawson. "It's not anywhere near as bad as you're thinking."

He stared at her without speaking. Words seemed to have escaped him, and he feared saying the wrong thing to her. Instead, he nodded and watched her walk away.

Once she had left the room, Dawson moved his gaze to McAllister's. "I believe it's time I left. I have some things I need to attend to." He tried to walk by the general but the older man reached out and grabbed his arm.

"Oh, no, you don't. We need to have a long talk about that little lady who just left here."

"And just what would you like to speak of, General?"

"Like the fact that she's done nothing but talk about you since we picked you up off that planet. Or how about the fact that she's in love with you, even if she hasn't said as much," McAllister replied. "Do I need to explain that she's not suited for military life? I assigned her to your ship on this research trip because I thought she would be safe. She insisted on going on a mission. What else could I do?" He sighed and ran a hand through his hair.

"When we lost contact with you and the SOS came in, I was worried. Then we began receiving the emergency signal, you have no idea what I was going through. But I always had faith that you would keep her safe." His gaze returned to Dawson. "She said you kept a cool head the entire time and did everything possible to keep everyone safe."

"I appreciate your confidence in me, sir," Dawson said. Another part of what the general had said played over and over in his mind, trying to find a place to sink in. Meredith loved him.

"What's the matter? Can't believe she loves you? Yes, I found that one rather hard to swallow myself. But she does. You can see it in her eyes when she looks at you, hear it in her voice when she talks about you," he explained. His face took on a serious expression. "Life is too short to let love pass you by. But do *not* break her heart." He hadn't added "*or else*" but it hung between them, almost tangible in the air.

"Sir, I have no intention of doing any such thing. She claimed my heart the moment she boarded ship," Dawson confessed.

"Then let me make a suggestion."

Dawson nodded, shrugging his shoulders. "At this point, any help would be most welcome."

"Tell her how you feel. She is scared to death you will leave her when we get back to the home world," McAllister told him.

"Now where in hell did she get a harebrained idea like that? She's more stubborn than what's good for her."

McAllister chuckled. "Looks like you already know more than you thought you did about Meredith. Go after her," the general replied with a shove to Dawson's shoulder.

Dawson left McAllister standing in the canteen chuckling and went to track Meredith down. If he had to guess on her whereabouts, he'd have bet money she was in her quarters, but when he got there, her rooms were empty. *Where was that woman?*

He went back to his own rooms. He'd access the computer from there and find her location. The room door slid open when he approached it. "Lights," he called out without missing a step. When the lights came on, he stopped dead in his tracks, his mouth dropping open. Meredith lay on his bed, naked as the day she was born, waiting for him.

"What the…"

Meredith smiled. "Didn't expect to see me here, did you?"

"How'd you get in? The door's programmed to open only for me," he said, glancing over his shoulder at the door.

"I, um, tampered with it a bit." She held up two fingers with just a small bit of space between them.

"Tampered, eh? And why does this *not* surprise me?"

She shrugged one naked shoulder as she waved a hand nonchalantly. "I don't know. Why doesn't it?" She slid her legs around to the bed's edge and stood.

He covered the distance between them in three long strides and pulled her roughly against him. Meredith's breath escaped her lips in a whoosh, her back arched as her head fell back. His blue eyes glittered down at her. She laughed, letting the need grow.

The fabric of his shirt felt rough against her breasts as she fought for breath. The hungry look in his eyes sent shivers racing down her spine and set her heart to pounding rapidly. She ached to feel his long shaft buried deep within her, longed to be joined with him in the most intimate of ways. "Make love to me, Dawson. I need you."

He didn't reply with words. His mouth crashed down on hers, his tongue darting between her lips to tangle with her own. Dawson slowly moved his hands over her naked form, enjoying the smooth, silky feel of her skin.

She watched him undress and move to her side. He was so handsome, from the top of his light brown-blond head to the bottoms of his big feet, but more importantly, he was all hers.

Meredith kissed him passionately then pulled her lips from his and planted a kiss in the center of his chest. Her tongue lapped over one flat, male nipple. Her teeth nipped at his skin. She curled her fingers around him, stroking him, rubbing her hand around the purple head, his cock pulsing under her touch.

He moved his hands into her hair, pulling her back up to his mouth. He moved forward, until her back pressed against the cool wall. Taking her by the hips, he lifted her and impaled her down on his shaft. Her warm, moist heat wrapped around him, surrounding him with the silky, smooth interior of her pussy. Pleasure gripped him tightly, refusing to relinquish its hold. He moved within her, slowly at first, then with rapidly increasing speed as he strove to build the tension higher and higher.

His only thoughts of completion, he drove into her harder and harder with each passing stroke, every thrust of his hips. Muscles rippled, bunched and pulled taut with the increase in passion, his breath came in gasps as he pumped to reach his goal. Something within him coiled and the tension broke, his seed spilling into her hot, slick sheath.

Meredith kissed his neck, gasping for breath, and her heartbeat pounded in her chest and ears. But she still wanted more.

"Dawson," she moaned against his throat. "More."

He chuckled, pulling himself from her and lowering her to the floor. "Come on, baby. I'll give you more." He took her hand, leading her into the bathroom, where he paused by the shower stall. "Shower."

The hot spray started and steam filled the room. "In you go," he urged, urging her into the stall before him. Taking the bar of soap in hand, he lathered her body, taking his time. He massaged her sore, well-used muscles with his hands, leaving a soapy trail in his wake. He pinched her nipples between his thumb and forefinger. Then he lowered his head, took one pert nipple into his mouth, tugging at it with his teeth. He fastened his tongue around it, sliding his free hand down to the heated folds of her pussy. Rubbing her clit, he waited for her to moan before pushing his fingers inside her, pressing deep against her hot spot, making her writhe against him.

"Do you want it slow or fast?"

"Fuck me hard." She hoped she didn't sound too eager, but she needed him desperately. Her body ached for more. She loved him. In such a short time, he had become her heart and soul.

"Gladly, love."

Dawson urged her to turn around, teasing her body as she did so. He pulled her hands up to the tiles and pressed them there, then spread her legs apart. His mouth continued to tease her neck and shoulder while his other hand moved down to slide between the rounded cheeks of her ass, rimming his finger around the puckered opening of her anus, gently pressing against it.

She thrust her ass back against him, enjoying the way his finger stretched her open for him. Her body ached and burned with need, and she loved the scraping of his teeth against her skin.

He played at her openings with his fingers, teasing first one, then the other until her knees threatened to buckle. She gasped when he pushed his fingers into her pussy, his thumb into her ass. Grasping the small bar behind the shower spray, she leaned further over, shoving her ass toward him in invitation. She was so aroused that she didn't care where he impaled her, just as long as he did. She needed him inside, and she wanted him now.

"Now, Dawson. Now."

He rubbed the tip of his hardened shaft against her pussy, along the crack of her ass. He pushed his hard cock inside her hot folds, only to withdraw.

She moaned in frustration, pushing back against him when he pulled out.

"Dawson, please," she cried.

He chuckled. Loving her was such fun. Again, he rubbed against her and shoved his thick cock into her pussy. This time, he didn't withdraw. He thrust his hips against hers, striving for fulfillment.

Meredith cried out in pleasure, enjoying the feel of his shaft moving within her. The hot water cascaded down her back and over her sensitive flesh, adding to the overwhelming jolts of pleasure. She shoved back against him, meeting him thrust for thrust, sliding him deeper with each stroke until the pleasure peaked and she convulsed around him. Ripple after ripple of pleasure washed over her as the contractions overtook her body.

Dawson's groan of pleasure reached her, but she was too exhausted, too sated to react to it.

Slowly, he withdrew from her, lifting her into his arms, he grabbed some towels—enfolded her tenderly then carried her out of the shower stall. "Off," he commanded, and then carried her from the room and to bed.

Chapter Twelve

ɛɔ

The tempest on Ferraven continued to grow, melding itself to into a malevolent force of nature. Lightning danced across the desert plains and ran along the underbelly of the storm as it grew in strength and intensity.

The sand vibrated, moved as if it had a life of its own. The winds kicked up, swirling the fine particles around, blending and mixing them until the rich colors ran together.

Another bolt of lightning cracked. A roll of thunder boomed and washed over the land—the very ground vibrated beneath its fury. As the heavens opened up and poured down on the desert, life was reborn.

The solidified heart of the beast shattered, the churning of the sand broke the tiny fragments apart until they blended with the rest, seamlessly, unnoticeable. The ground shook once more as the creature's mighty roar echoed across the plains. A deep depression formed in the middle of the desert, as if something sucked it down. It trembled and spun until a mass of sand spewed forth with a deafening roar and headed for the stars.

Its shape shifted as it took on yet another form. Sand turned to metal as long tentacles shot forth in every direction, a long, whiplike tail formed and massive jaws extended waiting to claim its victim. With his new form came new strength. He launched skyward, racing through the planet's atmosphere. It shot through space at an alarming speed, its crashed vessel left forgotten on the barren planet below.

He would find her, he would capture and kill her, and he would kill all who crossed his path.

They thought they had destroyed him, though all they had done was anger him further. His body spun with increasing speed as his anger flamed higher and higher. Time had passed, he knew not how much. But it made no difference. They were connected. He would find her and the others, and they would all be his—his to kill.

* * * * *

"You don't like Kaz, do you?" Meredith questioned, running her fingers over Dawson's chest.

"It goes back a long way, Meredith. From the beginning he was someone you couldn't get close to, someone you automatically disliked."

"So you did. He's not as bad as that, really. Not at all. You just have to get to know him."

Dawson leaned back to look at her face. "Get to know him? You're kidding, right?"

"Trust me, he's a very caring person."

"Honey, I don't doubt he is where you're concerned, but not just anyone can get that close to him. He's pretty much unapproachable, downright scary in fact," he confessed. "Ow!" Dawson rubbed his chest where she'd smacked him. "What was that for?"

"Kaz isn't scary."

"Not to you, but to the rest of us, he rates right up there with the devil himself," he assured her.

"That's not funny, Dawson." She rolled away from him. Climbing from the bed, she stalked across the cabin and jerked her shirt on, turning her back to him.

Dawson slid from the bed and moved up behind her. He held her close, circling his arms around her waist and resting his chin atop her head. "I'm sorry, baby. I never meant to hurt your feelings."

"He's not a bad person," she pointed out. "He took me in when I had no one else and made sure I was taken care of."

"How'd he do that? Now, don't go getting all huffy on me again," he said when he felt her tense again. "I'm just curious as to how he took care of you while he was off doing his duty."

"His late wife's family took me in. He loved her so much. It nearly killed him when he lost her, in fact, he still won't talk about it. I worry about him. He keeps too much bottled up inside."

"He'll talk when he's ready to, love. You can't always help people, no matter how badly you want to. Sometimes they have to help themselves." He kissed the top of her head and squeezed her tight against him. "Let me take care of you, and then maybe he will take care of himself and take the time to heal."

Meredith turned in his arms and looped her arms around his neck. "Are you trying to tell me something, Captain Lang?" She leaned back in his arms and smiled up at him.

"Haven't I said it yet?"

Meredith shook her head slowly.

"Hmm, guess I'll have to fix that then." He leaned forward and gently kissed the tip of her nose. Pulling back to see her eyes, he whispered, "I love you, Meredith Carson, and I want you by my side forever and always."

"Oh, Dawson," she sighed, squeezing his neck. "I love you so much." She feathered his face with kisses, making soft smacking noises in the quiet of the cabin. "I never dreamed you'd love me back."

"I never thought you'd love me. I'm more than a decade older, I'm a captain without a ship and have no idea what the future holds at this point."

"None of that matters, so long as we are together."

Dawson grinned and pulled her up against him. "That's what I like to hear."

Meredith laughed. Her head tipped back for his kisses.

As their lips touched, a loud crashing sound was heard and the entire ship shook with a tremendous jolt. Dawson's head jerked up, eyes darting around the room.

Meredith raised her hands to her temples, her eyes squeezed shut. "It's here."

"What's here? That thing? How in hell…"

"We didn't kill it. We just slowed it down," she told him.

"How do you know that?"

"I can feel it." She turned away from him, lest he see the fear in her eyes. "It's come for me."

"Well, the asshole can't have you," he sternly replied, pulling on his jeans. He brushed by her, buttoning his shirt, and stalked out the door into the corridor.

Meredith started to chase after him but paused at the door. With a heartfelt sigh, she glanced down at her bare legs. "Damn it."

* * * * *

Alarms sounded as people scurried about in the corridors on their way to their posts. The ship was under attack and panic reigned. Dawson fought his way through the harried people. He had to find McAllister. He had to inform the other man of what was happening.

He charged through the doors onto the bridge as the creature slammed against the ship with immense velocity. Barely maintaining his balance, he hurried to the general's side.

"Shields are up, sir," a crewman reported.

"What in the hell is that thing?" Kaz demanded, staring at Dawson.

"The people of the planet had called it a Kalerian, sir."

Kaz turned wide eyes on Dawson. "I thought you reported that it had been destroyed on the planet."

"I thought it had, but obviously I was mistaken." He paused and ran a hand through his newly trimmed hair. "It's after Meredith."

"Like hell it is," McAllister growled. "Ensign, fire everything we've got at that son of a bitch. Blow it out of space."

"Yes, sir," the crewman replied, pressing the emblems on the screen before him.

The creature was unfazed by the shots. Dawson let out a sigh and ran his hand through his hair again. "Damn it. This isn't working, but I think I know what will." He took off out the door before McAllister could question him.

"Shit! Anderson, you're in control," he ordered. "She'll kill me if anything happens to him." He spun and chased after Dawson. "Where in hell are you going?"

"Landing bay."

"Why?"

"I'm going to lure that thing away." Dawson never looked back. He moved on through the panicking people.

"This is insane. Do you really think your sacrifice will make her feel any better if you end up dead? Have some common sense, man. There's got to be another way."

Dawson entered the bay and moved to one of the small ships held inside. He turned his attention back to McAllister. "I never said I was killing myself. Have a little faith, General. Give me some credit for having some intelligence."

"That has yet to be seen," McAllister scoffed.

Dawson gave him a wry grin. "Once I get inside and I'm ready, open the bay doors. We've got one chance to draw this thing away and I don't intend to waste it."

"What if he doesn't follow?"

"He will," Dawson stated without doubt.

"Once he does, what happens then?"

"I end this game once and for all." He stepped into the ship and closed the door.

McAllister stood staring after him, shocked that Dawson had walked away before he could finish his argument. Moving to the control room, he waited for Dawson's signal.

"Ready, McAllister. Open her up."

McAllister reached out and ran his fingers along the scanner, causing the bay doors to open. Dawson eased the ship out and away from the *Phoenix*. He powered down and waited for the creature to appear.

Above the larger ship, he saw the flash of what looked like a large tentacle. Dawson smiled. "Time for payback." He maneuvered around the *Phoenix* until he had the creature in his sights. Dawson fired at the beast, and had to bite back a cry of victory when the shot hit its mark.

The creature roared and spun on the tiny vessel attacking it as Dawson watched through wide eyes. He waited until the Kalerian was almost upon him, before quickly turning the ship and heading out into space away from the *Phoenix*.

He jolted forward in his seat at the impact of the creature attacking. Long, thick metal tentacles wrapped around the ship, obscuring his view. He punched another button and extended the research arms, clamping down on the creature, holding it to the ship. Dawson hoped it would be unable to shift its form while in space.

He prepared the autopilot. Then, he pointed the ship toward a star and punched it to full throttle. It may have survived a metal rod through the heart and being struck by lightning, but surely to God there was no way it could survive the incinerating heat of the sun.

Just beyond the gravitational pull of the star, he switched on the autopilot, climbed into the escape pod and hit the eject button. Nothing happened.

"Oh, shit!" He pressed the button again, then spun around and broke out the glass on the manual release. "Oh, fuck," he muttered, pulling at the release handle. The damn thing was jammed. "No, oh, please, no. Don't do this to me now."

He squeezed his eyes tightly shut and pulled with all his strength, Meredith's voice whispering softly in his mind. The release handle finally gave way, causing him to fall back from the force he exerted.

Regaining his senses, he spun back around and sent the pod off, away from the ship. He watched, with a growing sense of relief, as the ship grew smaller and smaller, until it disappeared from sight.

Dawson swallowed hard as he waited, watching his onboard scanner. When the other ship disappeared off the scanner, he steered the small craft back toward the coordinates where the *Phoenix* had been.

Chapter Thirteen

 හ

"Where is he? Where is he, Kaz?" Meredith demanded as she flew into the landing bay. The men on the bridge had told her where to find them.

"He's not here."

"Then where is he?" she asked, a sudden feeling of dread washing over her.

"Out there," Kaz replied, pointing toward the bay doors.

"Oh, God." She ran into the control room and started to work on the control panel. The events occurring outside the ship popped up on a screen and Meredith's breath jerked in.

That tiny ship covered by the monster held Dawson, her man, her life. If anything happened to him because of her...no, she couldn't think like that. He'd be fine, just fine, and once he got back on ship, his ass was in so much hot water it wasn't even funny.

She watched the long-distance scanner display in horror as the small ship turned toward the nearby sun and drove straight into the turbulent surface. "No!" she screamed, collapsing onto the floor.

Kaz ran to her side and knelt down. "Honey, he's fine. The escape pod was launched from the ship. He's on his way back now."

"He can't be gone. He can't be," she cried. "I'd feel it if he was gone."

He shook her hard. "Meredith, listen to me! He's not gone. He should be back any minute. As soon as the pod is close enough, the tractor beam will pull him in."

She looked up at him with tear-filled eyes. "You promise?"

"I'd never lie to you about something so serious."

They sat there on the floor until they heard the bay doors open. Kaz looked at her and smiled. "See, I told you. Those doors will only open for a ship programmed with the access code for the *Phoenix*."

Meredith climbed to her feet with Kaz's help and watched the small ship drift into the landing bay. The large, metallic doors slid closed behind it with a loud thud. It was all she could do to contain herself. She wanted to feel him in her arms, to reassure herself that he was truly okay.

"Happy?" Kaz asked.

"Not yet, but I will be."

She paced the floor of the control room. The minutes ticked by as if they were hours and her nerves were nearly shot when the ship finally docked.

As soon as the landing bay had been stabilized and it was safe for her to leave the control room, she ran through the doors and rushed to the ship. She watched impatiently as the pod's doors slowly opened and Dawson walked down the ramp.

She felt a smile curve her lips at the sight of him and she flung herself into his arms as soon as he cleared the ramp. "If you ever pull another stunt like that, Dawson Lang, I will hurt you myself," she warned between kisses.

"Worried about me, were you?" he chuckled. "Does a man good to know he's loved."

She pulled back and swatted his arm. "You knew that before you pulled this harebrained stunt. And if you ever do it again—"

He reached out, wrapped an arm around her waist and pulled her back into his arms. "I'm hoping there's never a need for a repeat performance, Meredith. Shut up and kiss me."

Meredith pressed her lips to his, opening wide to allow him entrance into her mouth. Her tongue danced with his as she snaked her arms around his neck, her body pressing closer.

"Ahem!" sounded behind them, breaking them apart.

Meredith blushed as she glanced over at Kaz. "Sorry."

"Uh-huh, sure you are." He glared at the two of them before cracking a smile. "Get the hell out of here and find a room. I'm really not into watching my niece being ravished by a space cowboy."

Meredith laughed as she moved toward him. Going up on tiptoe, she kissed his cheek. "I don't really care to have you watching, either, Kaz. Dawson? I'll be waiting…"

She walked past him and out of the landing bay without looking back. She knew Dawson would soon follow. *Then* she'd show him just how much she loved him, no matter what it took.

* * * * *

Dawson shrugged and gave McAllister a lopsided grin. "Women, go figure."

"Captain," he laughed. "My advice to you would be to look for more private quarters and follow—follow quickly. She's impatient and won't be happy if you make her wait."

Dawson's mind went back to earlier when he'd found her waiting for him in his cabin. "Thanks for the advice, sir, sorry to rush, hafta go." He smiled secretly as he passed by the general and headed off after Meredith.

Which cabin would she be in this time? His? Hers? He'd try his first. If she wasn't there, then he'd just clean himself up and make her wait a bit longer. A little wait never hurt anyone.

When he arrived at his door, he found the cabin empty. He entered his quarters and headed straight for the bathroom. Shower, shave and then he'd go looking for her. By then, she should be good and ready for him.

He stripped off his clothes as he crossed the room. Just the thought of hot water running down his body felt good. After the encounter with the Kalerian, he was sure he didn't smell very good. Lord knew he'd sweated enough and he wasn't going to go to Meredith smelling ripe.

"Shower," he called out, entering the small room. He stepped beneath the hot spray and sighed.

He rotated his shoulders as the water pelted his skin. Placing his hands on the cool tile, he leaned forward and allowed the water to run down his back and legs.

Dawson lifted his face into the spray. The hot water stung, but it helped to relieve the tension in his body. He leaned his forehead against the cool tiles, his hand moved up to caress his flaccid penis.

Visions of a nude Meredith danced in his head and he felt his cock harden. His hand stroked the hard length before he groaned and released his hold. He banged his head against the tiles.

"Damn it. Here I am jacking off when Meredith's in her cabin waiting for me. What in hell am I thinking? I'm a moron!" he growled at his dim reflection in the shower door. "Shower off."

He stepped from the stall and dried himself before padding out to pull on clean clothes. As the last button slipped into its hole, he stepped into his boots and left whistling, in search of Meredith.

* * * * *

Meredith paced her cabin in the nude. "Where in the hell is he? He knew I'd be waiting."

She went to the small replicator on the wall and scrolled through the selection list. There were enough female officers onboard the *Phoenix*. They had to have something she could use.

"There!" she exclaimed when she found the database for self-pleasure instruments. "Good lord, how many pages of this stuff is there?" The list seemed to go on forever.

"Let's see. There's the bullet, single and double, a G-spot vibe, a hydra vibe, jelly vibe, ecstasy balls, and the genie," she read off, just to name a few. "Holy shit, this list goes on forever." She reached out and tapped the screen, selecting a strawberry-scented lubricant and a jelly vibe. "Hmmm, I guess I want a purple one, eight inches long."

She finished typing in the info and touched the replicate button. Instantly, the accessories appeared inside the compartment. She reached in, pulled them out and smiled. "Who says you gotta have a man?"

Crawling onto the bed, she grabbed up her new vibe and screwed the lid off the bottle of lubricant. The sweet aroma of strawberries wafted up and teased her nostrils as she squeezed out a generous portion into her hand. The liquid was cold and sticky, and she giggled at the feel of it in her palm. Holding the vibe in her other hand, she rubbed the lubricant all over its length and then licked her hand.

"Mm, that's not half bad." She placed the bottle next to the lid then situated a pillow behind her back. Leaning back, she faced the door she'd programmed to only open at her or Dawson's command.

Meredith spread her legs wide, turned on her toy and played at her clit using the fingers of one hand. A moan escaped her lips when thrills of pleasure shimmered through her body. She pinched the sensitive nub before sliding the vibe inside her aching pussy.

Her free hand moved up to twist her nipples into tight little crowns. She wished desperately it was Dawson's hard cock driving deep within her instead of the vibe, his mouth at her breast instead of her hand. Slowly, she began moving it in and out of her tight sheath. Her eyes fluttered closed, and she imagined Dawson's large frame looming over her, his cock moving in and out of her in an agonizingly hard, slow rhythm.

The more she moved, the faster her movements became, until she found herself standing on the threshold of release. Her back arched when the first ripple of pleasure shot through her. Another moan spilled from her throat.

A beeping noise sounded in the background. Meredith gasped when she realized it was the sound of the door opening and Dawson stood there, wide-eyed with shock.

She giggled huskily and held out a hand to him. "Join me, Dawson. Make me feel like only you can."

He raised an eyebrow at her uninhibited show. "You seem to be doing pretty good on your own."

She groaned in frustration.

He watched her wiggle under his gaze, her body enticing him to join her. His cock had hardened the instant he'd walked in the door and caught a glimpse of what she was doing. Meredith lying naked on the bed in the throes of passion was a glorious sight if he'd ever seen one. And he wanted nothing more than to join in on her pleasure.

Without another second's hesitation, he stripped off his clothing and reached for her.

Meredith shook her head. "Not yet."

"Why not?" Hell, he wasn't sure he could wait. He wanted her and he wanted her now.

"I want to do something for you first." She squirmed again as the vibrator hit a particularly sensitive spot. "Sit over the top of me, Dawson, and get just as close as you can."

He climbed onto the bed and straddled her, inching his way up until she seemed satisfied. *Those are orders I don't mind taking.*

She smiled wickedly and her hand reached up to wrap around his hard cock. "Closer," she murmured.

He inched a little closer then moaned in pleasure when her mouth encircled his dick.

She slid her tongue down the hard length, pressing against the thick, purple vein along its underside. She sucked with increasing and decreasing pressure, moving her mouth up and down his shaft.

He slipped his hands into her hair, holding her to him. "Oh, God, baby, harder. That feels so good."

He moved his hips back and forth in time with her rhythm. When her free hand traced up the outside of his thigh then wrapped around to clutch at his ass, he groaned and rotated his hips, pressing into her mouth even more.

"Don't stop, Meredith. Oh, please don't stop."

She dug her nails into his ass cheeks, then slid around and cupped his balls. She squeezed and massaged in time to the movement of her mouth. She smiled, enjoying the way he moved and the sounds he made.

The pressure within him built with each stroke of her lips, the squeeze of her hand. Her tongue swirled around his sensitive tip, an electric sensation shot through him. "Oh, baby, I'm going to come." He tightened his grip in her hair. "Stop or get a mouthful."

Meredith didn't listen to his warning. Back and forth she moved with his hips, sucking, licking and teasing. He burst into her mouth moments later, and she swallowed his come as fast as she could. The hot, sticky liquid leaving a salty taste on her tongue as it slid down her throat. Her hand continued to massage his balls as her tongue moved over his tip, removing all traces of his seed.

Pulling back from her, he bent down and captured her lips. The salty taste of his seed clung to her lips.

She opened up to him, allowing him access into the hot, moist confines of her mouth. His tongue slid inside and danced with her own. She moaned in pleasure at the way his tongue twisted and mated with her own.

"Oh God, baby, that was sooo...good," he repeated against her lips.

"Turnabout is fair play," she whispered.

He slid from the bed and turned to look down at where she lay, back against the pillows. A large purple vibrator continued to move within her—he envied the piece of pulsating jelly its spot within her warm body.

Grabbing her by the hips, he turned her around, until she sat on her knees. Reaching for her bottle of lube, he squeezed out a generous amount into his hand and smeared it over her ass, between her cheeks, and circled and dipped into the puckered opening to her anus.

He inhaled deeply. "Strawberry. My favorite."

Meredith chuckled. "I know. Now, hurry! I need you," she sighed. The vibe continued to move deep, sending continuous pulses rippling through her pussy.

Dawson wrapped his fingers around the hard length of his shaft. He pressed the tip to heated flesh near the purple vibe, enjoying the vibrations coursing through him. He groaned at the way it felt to have her flesh and the jelly exterior of the toy pulsing against his penis.

He then rubbed the tip over her ass and around the puckered flesh of her opening. His eyes closed and he groaned again while he continued to rub against her, teasing her until she moved back against him demanding more.

His free hand slapped her ass playfully, a loud, smacking sound echoing along with the soft hum of her vibrator. Pressing the head of his cock against her opening, he pushed forward, watching the tip slowly disappear into her.

Once the head was fully in, he paused to savor the feel of her tight heat surrounding him. His head fell back and he sighed deeply, enjoying the vibrations seeping into his body from hers.

It was a total bombardment of the senses. The smell of strawberries assaulted his nostrils. The sound of her gasps and the hum of her toy echoed in his ears, the feel of her hot channel gripping his cock.

He grasped her hips and pulled her back against him, inch by slow inch. His eyes opened as he watched her absorb the hard length of his cock until his balls were pressed against her vibrator.

His body shook in response to her toy. He paused a moment to take in this new, wildly arousing sensation. *Hot damn!* He'd keep this in mind for future occasions.

Withdrawing, he pulled back until only the tip of his penis remained within her then he pulled on her hips, slammed deep into her with enough force to jolt the air from her lungs. He fucked her slowly then fast, over and over again. He felt his come ready to erupt and tried to slow down. But the feel of her rocking rhythmically, meeting him thrust for thrust, and the strong clamp of the muscles of her ass, made it nearly impossible as she moved against him, pushing, pulling, grinding each time he got close. He prayed for the stamina to hold out until Meredith climaxed.

The tension within her body broke when he pushed into her, pinching and rolling her clit. The walls of her anus clenched and released repeatedly, leaving her quivering in the aftermath of such heated lovemaking.

Dawson followed right along behind her, plunging headfirst into ecstasy as his orgasm overtook him with enough force to steal his breath. His seed gushed out, filling her while it poured from his body. He gasped for breath, reveling in the sated exhaustion that washed over him.

Dawson withdrew from her and slid beside her on the bed. He pulled her into his arms, pushing the hair back from her forehead. "I love you," he whispered, feathering kisses along the length of her neck. He reached down, turned off the vibe and slid it from her hot, wet sheath.

She wiggled against him, spooning, finding the position where they fit perfectly together. "And I love you, Dawson. Always and forever."

Chapter Fourteen
Four days later
Zyphon III Spacestation

ℰℭ

Dawson stood before the mirror in his cabin adjusting his tie. "Are you sure this is necessary? I really hate these uniforms."

"I know you do," Meredith replied, reaching around him to help with the tie. "But this is a special occasion. You can't go to an awards ceremony dressed in your old jeans."

He spun around to face her. "But I like my outdated jeans. These uniforms are itchy and fit too tight."

She rolled her eyes at him. "Those jeans you wear are pretty tight as well."

"Oh, really?"

"Yep, they outline that fine ass of yours quite nicely."

He stepped closer and gazed down into her eyes. "If this thing didn't start in just a few minutes, I'd turn you over that table and have my way with you. Think about it, we could miss this ceremony and have a little private party just for you and me."

"Promises, promises," she sighed. "I have to go, Dawson. I have to get ready. I'll meet you in the Assembly Hall just before it starts." She went up on tiptoe and kissed him. "Don't change."

He sighed. "Okay, I won't. I promise. But as soon as this shindig's over, I'm out of this uniform."

"Fair deal." She smiled at him one last time, and then disappeared down the hall.

"The things I do for that woman," he muttered, grabbing his dress jacket. He shrugged into it and took off toward the Assembly Hall. Maybe if he arrived early, they'd start ahead of time, move through it quickly and he could get back into something less formal. Why they wanted to give him a medal for what happened on that godforsaken planet was beyond him.

"Lang," a voice called out as he stepped into the room where a small gathering had already formed.

He nodded while tugging his collar. "General. All this for me?" he asked. The whole situation made him uncomfortable.

General McAllister smiled. "All this is for you, and Meredith, of course. She was on the planet too."

"What about Hanson and Timmons?"

McAllister shook his head. "They shipped out this morning on a new assignment. Said to tell you they were sorry to be missing the special occasion."

Hell, it's just an award, I can get through this. He tugged at his collar—again. "Yes, they'll be missed. How were they?"

"Good as new. If not for the haunted looks they sometimes get, you would never know anything happened to them," McAllister replied.

"It wasn't a pleasant experience. That's for sure. Meredith's handling it very well, though."

"That is because she has you, Lang. You make her forget all about what happened on that planet and she sees only the good. Just be sure she's what you want or you'll answer to me."

Dawson smiled. "She's exactly what I want, but she's still got another three and a half years in service."

McAllister clapped him on the shoulder. "Don't worry so much. All will work out in the end."

* * * * *

Meredith pulled the frilly white dress over the top of her head and straightened it over her hips. She brushed her hair back and fastened it at the sides with clips.

"Dawson, my man, you are in for one hell of a surprise." She smiled at her reflection, grabbed up the single long-stem purple rose on her table and headed out the door.

She ran down the corridor toward the Assembly Hall. It was due to start any minute and she didn't dare to be late. If Dawson figured out what they were up to, the shit would really hit the fan. She really didn't think he'd take to being tricked like this, regardless of Kaz's reassurances.

The door came into view much quicker than she'd realized. She paused outside it and swallowed hard to remove the lump in her throat. He'd be angry, she just knew it.

With a deep breath, she stepped up to the door causing it to slide open. Meredith stepped inside and paused, allowing her gaze to travel over the room. A smile curved her lips upward at the corners when she spotted him.

He was so tall. Why hadn't she noticed that before? He stood a good several inches taller than those around him. Dawson looked stunning in his uniform, even though she knew he hated wearing it.

With another deep, calming breath, she moved through the crowd, people moving out of her way. She caught sight of Dawson and watched as he lifted his head, smiled and nodded in her direction. Even from the distance of half the room, she could see the sparkle in his eyes. *Love.* She saw love shining in his eyes.

She wiped her sweaty palm on her skirt and moved to his side. He smiled down at her — she smiled nervously in return. So far, so good.

Kaz walked up and hugged her. "Ready?"

"As ready as I am going to be," she whispered.

Kaz nodded. "If you two will follow me up front, we will get this party started."

Dawson's gaze moved over Meredith. She seemed anxious and, as far as he knew, that dress wasn't a regulation uniform. Where had he seen a dress like that before?

Before his mind could process his memories, he stood before the crowd with Meredith at his side.

"Ladies and gentlemen. We are here today to celebrate the bravery of one man and one woman. Captain Dawson Lang and Doctor Meredith Carson, for your bravery and courage, we present to you these medals of honor for outstanding acts of bravery in a dire situation," General K.C. McAllister said in a deep, booming voice.

Meredith closed her eyes and breathed in slowly. *Geez, that sounds so lame. Is that the best Kaz could come up with?* Dawson was going to figure this out any minute and walk out on her. She just knew it.

The medals were pinned to the front of their clothing. Then the general turned back to the assembly. "We also have a surprise for the good captain. The loss of a ship is difficult for any captain to take, but in this case, it was a tragedy that shouldn't have happened. With that said," he remarked, turning to Dawson and handing him a rolled-up piece of paper, "I present you with this."

Dawson took the scroll and unrolled it. "What the..." he gasped. On the paper were the plans for the *Drigon II*. "You're going to rebuild her?"

"Yes, Captain, we are. Consider her a gift for all the good you have done for the Alliance."

"Thank you, sir. I have no idea what to say."

"Then say nothing. It will be a few months before she is done, but rest assured that as soon as she is complete, the *Drigon II* is all yours. No strings attached." The general turned back to the crowd and smiled broadly. "I understand that we have a wedding ceremony to hold."

Meredith nearly fell through the floor when Dawson turned his blue gaze on her. She winced, covered her face with her hand then peeked up at him through her fingers. "Sorry?"

"Sorry?" He shook his head. "Meredith, it would have been nice to know what you were up to."

She pointed at Kaz. "Don't look at me. It was all his doing."

Kaz grinned broadly and walked up close to the pair. Leaning in so no one else could hear, he said through his teeth, "You're sleeping with her so you're going to marry her. Got it?"

Dawson smiled. "No objections from me, sir. But she's still in service."

Kaz shook his head. "Not anymore. I have a few favors owed me. If she wants out, she's out."

Both men turned to look at her. She swallowed. "Don't look at me like that."

"Do you want out?" Kaz asked.

She gazed up at Dawson and the expectant look on his face, then back to Kaz. She nodded. "I want out."

"Then consider it done. Now, let's get this party started," he shouted, shaking a fist in the air.

The crowd whooped and hollered through the entire ceremony so loudly, Meredith could barely hear the general's words. But when Dawson turned to face her, smiled and kissed her, none of that seemed to matter anymore. She was his.

"You're mine now, Mrs. Lang."

* * * * *

Meredith locked their cabin door behind her and leaned against the cool metal. She smiled at Dawson. "So, any plans, Mr. Lang?" she asked huskily.

"Maybe a few."

She nodded toward the little white box he held in his hand. "What's in the box?"

He held it up on his palm. "What? This box?" He glanced at the package and back up at her. "Oh, it's just a little something I made for you."

Meredith pushed away from the door and slowly crossed the room, smiling all the while. She sat down on the bed beside him and took the small white square in her hands.

She lifted her eyes to his. "What is it?"

"Open it and find out," he replied, tapping the lid.

She laughed. "Okay, I will." Carefully, she pulled off the top and gasped in surprise. She raised her eyes to his, catching the mischievous sparkle in their blue depths. "Think you're funny, don't you?"

"What?" He tried to look innocent, but she wasn't buying it. "I thought it was a very practical gift."

Meredith shook her head. "His and hers holo-shades? Dawson! Geez."

He chuckled. "What? You don't like them?" He ran his finger over the dark shades marked "his". "I thought we could try them out. They're already linked together. You won't even have to exercise your hacking skills."

She playfully swatted his arm. "No, I don't believe we'll be trying these out just yet. I was thinking more along the lines of the real thing for our first time as a married couple."

Dawson nodded. "That's understandable." He took the shades from her and placed them on the bedside table. "So, how would you like to do this, Mrs. Lang? Top, bottom, sideways, upside down? Your pick."

Meredith laughed. "You are such a nut."

"And you're just noticing this? Why, I'm shocked, Mere. I'd have thought that would have been one of the first things you'd noticed."

She shook her head and cupped his face between her palms. "Just shut up and kiss me already."

Meredith moved into his arms, tilting her head back for his kisses. He trailed kisses down the length of her neck, and she smiled as she held him close.

"Dawson..."

"Mm..."

"Give me a baby," she whispered.

"A baby? Now?" he asked, flabbergasted by her request.

"You know, a tiny human? And yes, now."

"How about this. Give me one year to get us started on our new life then we'll talk about it again."

Meredith pouted. He ran his finger over her pouty lips. "I'm not saying no. In fact, I'd love to have a baby with you, but I want us to be settled into a new life first. Hell, I don't even have a ship yet."

She kissed him on the nose. "Okay, cowboy, I'll hold you to that."

Epilogue
One year later
Aboard the Drigon II

ഔ

Dawson ran his hand over the leather-covered captain's chair. He had to admit, the engineering crew had done one hell of a job recreating the *Drigon*. The ship was just as beautiful as her predecessor. He watched Meredith roam around the bridge, inspecting the new controls and panels.

Carefully, he lowered himself down into the new chair, testing it out. It felt right...just right, in fact. He looked down at it, a question forming in his mind. "Is this my old chair?"

Meredith's giggle floated to his ears. "Yes, it is. Noticed that, did you? Kaz sent a team back to the planet on a recovery mission. The engineers used as much of the old ship as they could to create the new. What wasn't salvageable was melted down and used in the mix for the hull."

"And you didn't let me in on this because?"

She shrugged and perched herself in his lap. "Because it was a secret."

"Did any of you stop to think it might have been unsafe to return to the planet?"

She shook her head. "Nope. It was perfectly safe. After you killed the Kalerian, there was no threat left on the planet."

"And just how do you know that?"

"The dreams."

Dawson sat up straight, nearly knocking her off his lap. He pulled her back up against him and gazed into her eyes. "You're still having the dreams? Why didn't you tell me?"

She leaned forward and kissed him softly. "Because, they are just dreams. I'm not having the nightmares anymore. The dreams are more like a look into the past. He was the only one, Dawson. He didn't need his ship to get off the planet when he chased us because it wasn't his ship. It was his prison. When it crashed, he was set free and he killed all those people, an entire race, for no other reason than the sheer thrill of it."

"I'm not so sure I like you being a history viewer in your dreams like this anymore. Why couldn't he have targeted someone else?" he grumbled.

"Umm, maybe for the same reason you didn't pick anyone else." She struck a dramatic pose and tossed her hair over her shoulder. "I *was* the only female on the planet."

Dawson straightened out his legs, causing Meredith to slide down them and land on the floor. "Oh, please forgive me, your grace. It was an accident. I didn't mean to dump such elegance off onto the floor."

She raised one of her eyebrows and glared up at him. "That's not funny, Dawson."

He smiled and leaned over to help her up. "Oh, but I think it is."

"It is not, and here I was about to offer to help you break in your new chair." She stood without his help, dusting herself off.

"But it's not a new chair." He glanced at it then back at her. "Then again, does that really matter?"

"Well, it didn't."

"Didn't?" he asked, pouting for effect.

"You did just dump me off onto the floor." She pointed to the floor as if he'd already forgotten the incident.

Dawson dropped down to his knees at her feet. "Forgive me?"

"I might, it just depends, though."

"On what?"

"Remember that talk we had about babies?"

"Yes," he slowly replied.

"I took the antidote for my birth control today."

"You did?"

She nodded. "Uh-huh. Interested?"

"In?"

"Making a baby, silly. What else?"

He jumped to his feet and pulled her into his arms. "Ready and willing, baby."

He kissed her hungrily, moving his hips against hers. A noise sounded from one of the panels and he reluctantly lifted his head.

"Oh, what is it now? We're on the ship by ourselves. Who could it possibly be?"

They moved to the communications center and Dawson pushed the flashing button on the touch screen.

The cover on the communications monitor slid open and Kaz's image appeared before them.

"Meredith, Lang," Kaz said with a nod.

"Hi, Kaz. How are you?" Meredith smiled.

"I'm fine, dear. We're about to head out, but I wanted to see how Lang likes the ship and how things are going for the two of you."

"The ship is a beauty, sir, and again I must thank you for this."

"No need for thanks, and you can call me Kaz. I'm not in service anymore."

"You're a Ranger, and that to me means you're still in service." Dawson pulled Meredith to him, holding her close. "You said you were about to ship out. New assignment?"

"Yes, new assignment. We're heading out to the planet Zyrlon and will be out of touch until we've finished up there, that's why I'm communicating now."

"Zyrlon." Meredith repeated and smiled. "You're going to see the cheetahs, aren't you?"

"Shh, we're not supposed to talk about that."

"Oh," she replied. "Sorry. I didn't hear a word."

Kaz laughed. "That's my girl. Captain, take care of her or we'll have a serious discussion when I get back."

Dawson looked down at Meredith. "Sir, I've been taking care of her for the past year and I'll keep on taking care of her until I draw my last breath. Her and the kids, that is."

"Kids?" Kaz remarked. "Meredith?"

She laughed. "No, not yet, but we plan to remedy that very soon."

Kaz looked behind him as alarms sounded off in the background. "Look, I have to go, the departure alarms are sounding. I'll be in touch. Take care you two and don't overdo it, Meredith. Let me know how things work out."

"Will do, Kaz. See you soon, I hope."

He smiled and the screen went black.

Dawson hugged her tighter, patting her shoulder. "He'll be fine, love. He knows what he's doing." He chuckled. "I still can't believe he retired from the Alliance after we got married. I'd have thought he'd die in service."

"He said since he no longer had to watch over me, he really had no reason to stay enlisted. But you know Kaz, he couldn't stay inactive for long. I think the Rangers may be good for him."

"I understand how he feels. Shipping was my life before the military, and now it can be again. I only did my time in the service because of the wars." He pulled her back into the circle of his arms. "Besides, I have a wife now, and as soon as I get her to bed to make it, we'll have a little one on the way."

"You're not mad about the reversal?"

He shook his head. "Nope, I'm not mad about the reversal. I think kids would be great and I ain't gettin' any younger."

Meredith looked around him at his chair. "So, wanna try out that chair of yours?"

"As if I'm really gonna say no."

"Good," she said with a smile.

She placed her small hands on his chest and pushed, causing him to fall into the chair in an unceremonious heap. He laughed, his heart feeling lighter than it had in a long time.

"Lights," she murmured. "Music."

He raised an eyebrow and gazed at her. What did she have in mind? The sultry notes filled the room and he watched Meredith begin to sway her hips in time with the rhythm.

Dawson scooted down in the chair, propping his elbow on the chair arm and leaning his chin against his hand. He spread his legs wide and relaxed, as much as possible, while she danced for him.

She moved her body in erotic ways, spinning, writhing, with the music. His cock grew painfully hard while he watched, enthralled by every little movement she made.

Piece by piece, she slowly removed her clothing until she stood before him completely nude and still dancing to the music. He groaned when she unexpectedly dropped to her knees at his feet and slid her hands up his thighs.

Oh, hell yeah. Of all the things he'd expected, this was the last.

He focused his full attention on her hands and what she was doing with them. She unhitched the snap of his pants and slid the zipper down. He grabbed hold of the chair arms gripping them so tight his knuckles went white.

She moved her fingers over his abdomen, the light pressure of them sliding over his skin only added to the tension in his body. When she snaked her hand beneath the waistband of his briefs, he shuddered and groaned again.

He lifted his hips, giving her room to pull his clothes down out of her way. She slid them down his legs and ran her hands over his bare skin. Dawson arched his back when she enveloped his erection with her mouth. She slid her tongue along the underside of his cock, and he shuddered in response.

* * * * *

Meredith secretly smiled while she played at his knees. She licked and sucked, teasing with her tongue all the while. She slid her hands up his inner thighs, cupping the weight of his balls in one hand. Teasing the skin just below them with one finger, she couldn't help but grin when he tensed beneath her touch.

She gently scrapped her teeth along his length, feeling him tense and shudder in reaction. With each reaction she received from him, her own need and desires grew in intensity. She was wet and more than ready to feel the hard length of his cock sliding into her.

"Mm," she moaned, sliding her lips over his skin.

"Meredith, darlin', you're killing me."

She lifted her head and look up at him with a smile. "Not yet, I'm not." She stood before him in nothing but that smile then climbed up onto his lap. "How's about we break this chair in right?"

He slid his hands up into her hair and fisted them there. "Sounds like a wonderful plan to me." He captured her lips with his own, delving his tongue into her mouth.

Meredith moaned and pressed her breasts into his chest as she lifted herself up enough to slide his hard length into her wet and ready pussy. She rocked her hips, matching the rhythm of his tongue sliding between her lips.

Pulling her head back, she rocked her hips harder, riding him in fast, deep strokes. Dawson's hands moved down to her hips and helped to guide her movements.

"That's it, baby. Ride me," he panted.

Meredith laughed when he groaned. She lifted her head and gazed down at him before wrapping her arms around his neck while he suckled her breasts. "Give me a baby, Dawson," she whispered at his ear.

He lifted his head and looked up at her with the funniest expression on his face. Before she could react, he stood and lowered them both down onto the floor.

The metal panels were cold against her back, but the warmth of his large body over her quickly made her forget all about it. He slid between her legs, pushing himself as deep as he could go into her body.

"Now say that again," he demanded.

"Say what?" she asked. "That I want a baby?"

"Yes." He held her head in his hands and stared into her eyes. "Say it."

"Give me a baby, Dawson."

He pulled back and thrust his hips forward. Meredith's head went back and her breathing became ragged as he moved over her, harder and faster with each stroke. She slid her hands along his sides and over his muscular back, enjoying the way the muscles rippled beneath her palms. Biting into his shoulder, she gasped for breath and dug her nails in as the tension within her built to the breaking point.

"I'm going to come, Meredith. Are you ready for it?" he breathed at her ear.

"Oh, God, yes!" she screamed as he thrust harder into her, and the tension within her broke as wave after wave of pleasure washed over her.

The strength of her orgasm shook her entire body as Dawson stiffened above her. He groaned sharply then collapsed onto her.

He lifted his head, panting for breath. "What do you bet you just got your wish?"

She pushed and he rolled over, taking her with him. Meredith smiled down at him and moved her hips. "And if we didn't, oh well. We'll just have to keep trying."

Dawson laughed and held her tight. She was so wonderful, and all his. He'd never thought himself a lucky man, but this last year with Meredith had proved him wrong. And to think, he hadn't even wanted her aboard his ship — what a fool he'd been.

Also by Heather Holland

The Beauty Within

About the Author

ဆ

Born and raised in the south, I'm about as southern as it gets. I've always loved to tell stories, but for some reason waited until I was grown and had my kids to start seriously writing. My husband is wonderful and very helpful when it comes to the things I write, even going so far as to help me figure out a plot line. I love writing paranormals, futuristics, contemporaries, and fantasies, because when my imagination is running free is when I'm happiest. Vampires, Lycans, and Cowboys—OH MY!

Heather Holland welcomes mail from readers. You can write to her c/o Ellora's Cave Publishing at 1056 Home Avenue, Akron, OH 44310-3502.

The Beauty Within

ℬ

Waves crashed upon the rocky shore with a deafening roar. Sea spray shot into the air to be carried away by the wind and spread across the isle.

Stone statues littered the beach and entranceway to the cavern. Their forms captured in numerous poses, their faces frozen in horror.

Where sand turned to rock, a cave opening loomed. The foreboding darkness warned all who dared stray ashore to stay back. A fate worse than death lingered in the shadows awaiting its next victim.

Beyond the beaches, nestled high on a hill, a decaying building rose toward the heavens. The thick, vine covered columns stood like towering sentinels in the moon's pale light.

A courtyard covered in cracked tiles lay at the bottom of broken marble steps. Shards of shattered glass hung in the windows and reflected the moon's iridescent light, sending it across the yard to reveal even more statues.

Deep within the crumbling structure, she dwelled hidden away from the light of day…the companionship of others. Doomed to spend an eternity alone, living in shadows.

Medusa looked into the reflective pool before her. The water revealed flawless skin and dark hair. Yet, the image was nothing more than a memory, for in reality she was a monster.

Now, her hair writhed as the snakes moved, her legs joined to form a long serpent's tail, and her features contorted until the very sight of her turned men to stone. Her once graceful hands were little more than a deadly collection of razor sharp claws.

Damn Athena's insane jealousy. If not for the interfering goddess, she would still be beautiful. Had she not allowed Poseidon to seduce her in Athena's Temple, she would not be cursed to inhabit such a horrendous form.

Anger welled up inside her. She slapped her reflection, sending a spray of water across the room. It was not fair. Why should she suffer while Poseidon went on as if nothing were wrong? All she wanted was to be loved. Hatred for the gods welled up within her, as well as sorrow at her situation.

Her serpents paused to study their queen. They knew her to be in distress, yet they did not know what to do.

Please help our mistress, the smallest serpent silently asked of the gods.

* * * * *

"The small one has requested our aid," Zeus remarked.

Hera nodded. "'Tis her destiny to find love. The Fates have told you as much." She stood beside him at the reflecting pool that revealed all on Earth. "Will you help her find her heart's desire?"

Zeus shook his head. "You know I cannot go against my own daughter, Hera. What would she think of her father?"

"No less than she thinks of you now. Athena has been able to care for herself since the day she was born. Do not worry over such petty things."

Zeus turned away. "I cannot. You can, if you must, but do not expect me to be of assistance. But you may only help her three times."

"I hardly think three times is enough to help this poor soul," Hera replied waving toward the reflecting pool.

"Three times, and certainly you can do it. You had only three with Jason, and he succeeded."

Hera pondered that a moment. "True." Sighing, she sat by the pool. "I do so think a storm would be quite lovely, especially if over the sea."

"You know I cannot. Poseidon rules the sea, not I."

"You are the king of all gods, are you not?"

Zeus's face reddened with rage. He furiously waved his hand over the pool, causing the sea to churn with the storm's fury as they watched.

"Happy? Though, I do not see what good a storm will do, and you are now down to two, my dear."

"Perhaps you did not pay close enough attention to the shore when you looked, and I am still at three."

Zeus stalked back to the pool and gazed at the wave beaten shore. A lone man washed ashore stumbling over the debris of his ship.

"What good will it do? Once he gazes upon her, he will share the others' fate." He began to leave the room. "And, Hera, you are now at two."

"Three Zeus, I did not ask for the storm, I merely stated one would be nice. You took it upon yourself to create it. As for our poor sailor, there is more to him than you see."

"His blindness does not change what she is or the impossibility of their union. The loss of his sight should count as one of your three."

"It is not my fault your storm resulted in his predicament. You are to blame for that not I, and it is still three."

"I will allow you your trickery this time, but do not let it happen again."

"As you command." She watched him walk away.

Hera's fingertips skimmed the water's surface. "Theron, brave and wise, find the gift I left upon the shore and give it to the lady of the isle. It will protect you, and enchant her." She watched him move toward the cavern.

Why an electronic book?

We live in the Information Age—an exciting time in the history of human civilization in which technology rules supreme and continues to progress in leaps and bounds every minute of every hour of every day. For a multitude of reasons, more and more avid literary fans are opting to purchase e-books instead of paperbacks. The question to those not yet initiated to the world of electronic reading is simply: *why?*

1. *Price.* An electronic title at Ellora's Cave Publishing and Cerridwen Press runs anywhere from 40-75% less than the cover price of the <u>exact same title</u> in paperback format. Why? Cold mathematics. It is less expensive to publish an e-book than it is to publish a paperback, so the savings are passed along to the consumer.

2. *Space.* Running out of room to house your paperback books? That is one worry you will never have with electronic novels. For a low one-time cost, you can purchase a handheld computer designed specifically for e-reading purposes. Many e-readers are larger than the average handheld, giving you plenty of screen room. Better yet, hundreds of titles can be stored within your new library—a single microchip. (Please note that Ellora's Cave and Cerridwen Press does not endorse any specific brands. You can check our website at www.ellorascave.com or

www.cerridwenpress.com for customer recommendations we make available to new consumers.)

3. *Mobility.* Because your new library now consists of only a microchip, your entire cache of books can be taken with you wherever you go.

4. *Personal preferences are accounted for.* Are the words you are currently reading too small? Too large? Too...**ANNOYING**? Paperback books cannot be modified according to personal preferences, but e-books can.

5. *Instant gratification.* Is it the middle of the night and all the bookstores are closed? Are you tired of waiting days—sometimes weeks—for online and offline bookstores to ship the novels you bought? Ellora's Cave Publishing sells instantaneous downloads 24 hours a day, 7 days a week, 365 days a year. Our e-book delivery system is 100% automated, meaning your order is filled as soon as you pay for it.

Those are a few of the top reasons why electronic novels are displacing paperbacks for many an avid reader. As always, Ellora's Cave and Cerridwen Press welcomes your questions and comments. We invite you to email us at service@ellorascave.com, service@cerridwenpress.com or write to us directly at: 1056 Home Ave. Akron OH 44310-3502.

Enjoy this excerpt from

The Beauty Within

© Copyright *Heather Holland 2003*

All Rights Reserved, **Ellora's Cave Publishing, Inc.**

THE
♱ ELLORA'S CAVE ♱
LIBRARY

Stay up to date with Ellora's Cave Titles in
Print with our Quarterly Catalog.

TO RECIEVE A CATALOG,
SEND AN EMAIL WITH YOUR NAME
AND MAILING ADDRESS TO:

CATALOG@ELLORASCAVE.COM

OR SEND A LETTER OR POSTCARD
WITH YOUR MAILING ADDRESS TO:

CATALOG REQUEST
c/o ELLORA'S CAVE PUBLISHING, INC.
1056 HOME AVENUE
AKRON, OHIO 44310-3502

erridwen, the Celtic Goddess of wisdom, was the muse who brought inspiration to storytellers and those in the creative arts. Cerridwen Press encompasses the best and most innovative stories in all genres of today's fiction. Visit our site and discover the newest titles by talented authors who still get inspired - much like the ancient storytellers did, once upon a time.

Discover for yourself why readers can't get enough
of the multiple award-winning publisher

Ellora's Cave.

Whether you prefer e-books or paperbacks,

be sure to visit EC on the web at
www.ellorascave.com

for an erotic reading experience that will leave you
breathless...